REX'S HONOR

THE AEGIS NETWORK: JACKSONVILLE DIVISION

JEN TALTY

JUPITER PRESS

PRAISE FOR JEN TALTY

"*Deadly Secrets* is the best of romance and suspense in one hot read!" *NYT Bestselling Author Jennifer Probst*

"A charming setting and a steamy couple heat up the pages in a suspenseful story I couldn't put down!" *NY Times and USA today Bestselling Author Donna Grant*

"Jen Talty's books will grab your attention and pull you into a world of relatable characters, strong personalities, humor, and believable storylines. You'll laugh, you'll cry, and you'll rush to get the next book she releases!" Natalie Ann USA Today Bestselling Author

"I positively loved *In Two Weeks*, and highly recommend it. The writing is wonderful, the story is fantastic, and the characters will keep you coming back for more. I can't wait to get my hands on future installments of the NYS Troopers series." *Long and Short Reviews*

"*In Two Weeks* hooks the reader from page one. This is a fast paced story where the development of the romance grabs you emotionally and the suspense keeps you sitting on the edge of your chair. Great characters, great writing, and a believable plot that can be a warning to all of us." *Desiree Holt, USA Today Bestseller*

"*Dark Water* delivers an engaging portrait of wounded hearts as the memorable characters take you on a healing journey of love. A mysterious death brings danger and intrigue into the drama, while sultry passions brew into a believable plot that melts the reader's heart. Jen Talty pens an entertaining romance that grips the heart as the colorful and dangerous story unfolds into a chilling ending." *Night Owl Reviews*

"This is not the typical love story, nor is it the typical mystery. The characters are well rounded and interesting." *You Gotta Read Reviews*

"*Murder in Paradise Bay* is a fast-paced romantic thriller with plenty of twists and turns to keep you guessing until the end. You won't want to miss this one..." *USA Today bestselling author Janice Maynard*

BOOK DESCRIPTION

Rex Jordan turned his back on a privileged life filled with country clubs and Ivy League education after a scandal involving his mother and his girlfriend's father shattered both their families. Leaving everything behind, Rex joined the Air Force, eventually aligning himself with a secretive group known as the Aegis Network in Jacksonville, Florida. He severed most ties with his family, yet when his estranged mother falls seriously ill and his past love arrives pleading for him to visit, Rex's life is thrown into turmoil. Faced with his mother's potential last wish and the return of his former love who once captured his heart, Rex must navigate his conflicting emotions.

Tilly Bettencourt, a woman who always followed her own path, refused to abandon her aspirations for Rex, causing their painful split. Now, with her father gone and Rex's mother near death, Tilly sees a chance to repair past damages and rekindle the intense connection they once shared. Will Rex open his heart again, or will old wounds prove too deep to heal?

NOTE FROM THE AUTHOR

Hello everyone!

It is important to note that this book was originally titled *Burning Kiss* and written as part of the Susan Stoker *Special Forces: Operation Alpha* world. Since the rights to the book have reverted back to me, I have stripped the story of all the elements from Susan's world (as it was legally required of me to do so) as well as changing the names of some of my characters so it would fit nicely into my Aegis Network series.

I have also expanded the story, adding scenes and updating a few things. I'm much happier with the storyline and characters now. I've always loved this series, but as with many things that I wrote years ago, I felt as though I could have done better.

Please enjoy!
Jen Talty

Everyone has a first kiss. But it's not always that first kiss that burns on our lips forever. This one is for my husband. My soulmate. To the man who captured my heart at eighteen and never let go.

WELCOME TO THE AEGIS NETWORK

The Aegis Network is the brainchild of former Marines, Bain Asher and Decker Griggs. While serving their country, Bain and Decker were injured in a raid in an undisclosed area during an unsanctioned mission. Instead of twiddling their thumbs while on medical leave, they focused their frustration at being sidelined toward their pet project: a sophisticated Quantum Communication Network Satellite. When the devastating news came that neither man would be placed on active duty ever again, they sold their technology to the United States government and landed on a heaping pot of gold and funded their passion.

Saving lives.

The Aegis Network is an elite group of men and women, mostly ex-military, descending from all branches. They may have left the armed forces, but the armed forces didn't leave them. There's no limit to the type of missions they'll take, from kidnapping, protection detail, infiltrating enemy lines, and everything in between; no job is too big or too small when lives are at stake.

As Marines, they vowed no man left behind.
    As civilians, they will risk all to ensure the safety of their clients.

The hot Florida sun beat down on the Intracoastal Waterway, dancing across the ripples conceived by a warm breeze rolling in off the salty ocean. Rex Jordan wiped away the perspiration beading across his forehead before he pulled back the throttles of his Absolute 50Fly luxury cabin cruiser, though others might consider it a yacht.

Rex called it home.

There was nothing better than living on the water.

"This has been an amazing day," Timothy White said. He stretched out on the seat behind the console. Timothy also worked for the Aegis

Network. He'd been the one to help open the Jacksonville Branch. He, his wife, and his kids were amazing people.

Rex glanced over his shoulder. Arthur had made himself comfortable on the stern bench, beer in hand, enjoying a day off from work at the station. Work at the Aegis Network. And work around the marina.

If Rex ever needed anything, Arthur would be at his side with the snap of his fingers. Men didn't come any better than him.

Even if Arthur had gotten him shot a few months back.

Rex rubbed his thigh, remembering the bullet tearing through his muscle. If he had to do it all over again, he'd gladly take the bullet since it had helped to save Arthur's wife and her mother.

They were good people.

Sitting around the table were the rest of the crew. The men he'd retired from the military with. The men he called family.

"Damn, and here we are back to reality," Timothy said. "Back where my twenty-year-old daughter thinks she knows more than me. A teenage son who's pushing boundaries, and two beautiful baby girls who think I'm the bomb. If it weren't for the little ones, I'd want to stay here forever, only my wife is itching for me to take her on a vacation. That means she wants another baby. I'm getting too old for this shit, but I want another one."

"As if you're actually bitching about your life," Rex said. "You love giving Mauve a hard time about her boyfriend, who you secretly love and want her to marry someday."

"Bite your tongue," Timothy said. "She's too young to be thinking about shit like that."

"He is a pretty cool kid." Kent waved his hand. "But I saw him and Mauve making out in Ruby's parking lot the other day. I had to cover my daughter's eyes, but not before she said, *look, Daddy, their sucking face.*"

"Shut up, asshole," Timothy said. "That's the last thing I want to hear."

"She's twenty fucking years old. Look at Kent; he had a kid at that age." Rex laughed. "And he's an excellent father. Most days."

"If you weren't at the helm, I'd deck you for pointing that out. That's my daughter." Timothy lifted his hand and waggled his finger over his head.

"If any of you assholes besides Kent knew what it was like to have kids, you'd understand."

"Trust me. I'm not looking forward to the day my baby girl tells me she has a boyfriend," Kent said. "Hell, I'm terrified of the day she wants a bra. I'm not equipped for that shit."

"Send her to Candice. She'll take her." Timothy chuckled. "She's the queen of shopping."

Rex once knew a girl who could do some serious damage with a credit card. Sadly, she'd been on his mind lately and he wished she wasn't.

"How's the baby making front, Arthur?" Buddy stood and stretched, twisting his body left and right. "Your wife with child yet?"

"Why is my sex life always the top of conversation in this group?" Arthur took a long sip of his beer. "Can we go back to busting Rex's balls? I prefer that so much better."

"I hope you have all girls." Timothy arched a brow. "Payback's gonna be a bitch."

"I think I'll remain single for a long while." Garth raised his beer. "I'm too young for this shit. Hell, I could be dating Ma—"

"I wouldn't finish that statement if I were you," Duncan interrupted. "You're nine fucking years older than Timothy's daughter. Too fucking old for her, and he'll put you in the ground."

"Just making a point that you all are old men." Duncan laughed.

"I'm only six months older than you, so fuck off," Kent said.

Hawke took his empty bottle and placed it in the recycle bin. "All I know is I've got a hot date with that waitress from last week."

"You've got a hot date every week," Arthur said. "No one can keep up with you."

"That's the fun part." Hawke waggled his brows. "I'm not ready to settle down."

Rex swallowed, hard. Once upon a time, he'd been madly in love. In fact, he'd been so far under the spell of a woman, he'd planned on getting married and having half a dozen rug rats. But now? The idea of even being around children made his skin prickle with fear. Not to mention, the idea of giving his heart to any woman made him want to rip it from his chest and stomp on it himself.

That would hurt less.

There hadn't been a woman in his life that hadn't hurt him. All starting with his mother. She'd ruined everything in his life, and now that she was dying, she wanted to reconcile.

Well, too late for that, Mom.

Rex navigated the cruiser through the docks at the marina Arthur's mother-in-law and wife owned. He put one engine in forward, the other in reverse, and turned the boat so he could back into his spot.

Arthur's wife, Maren, and Timothy's wife, Candice, stood at the end of the dock.

Maren was a beautiful woman with a great personality. She was perfect for Arthur. Kind, sweet, funny, intelligent, and she put up with all his friends as if they were family. He couldn't hate her if he tried.

And Candice. Holy shit. That woman cracked Rex up. It was impossible not to like her, and Rex tried to avoid being around anyone in a relationship, especially if they had kids. He could tolerate Mauve. She was an adult. And Xander, he was a cool teenager. Wise beyond his years. But the little ones? That was rough. It reminded him of all the broken promises and dreams.

Rex tapped the throttles in gear, then brought them to neutral.

Timothy slapped Rex on the back. "Thanks for this. But next time I'm bringing the whole family and we're staying for dinner."

"Only if Mauve brings her boyfriend." Rex

laughed, wishing Timothy could have stayed for dinner, but he knew he had a family to get back to. The only problem was Rex often ended up a third wheel with Arthur and Maren, which hadn't bothered him until recently. Seeing how happy Maren made Arthur reminded Rex of things past and for the first time in a long time, he felt a pang of loneliness.

A hint of regret.

A generous dose of resentment.

He'd lived alone since he left his parents' home twelve years ago, the summer between his junior and senior year of college. He didn't go back to school, and he hasn't been home since.

Not that he had a house to go home to since his father had sold it when his mother had left him for another man.

And his girlfriend chose her side.

"That can probably be arranged," Timothy said.

Rex shut off the engines, snagged the keys, and shoved them in the pocket of his jeans. He made his way to the stern of the boat, where Arthur and Maren had gathered, arms draped over each other, kissing. They were still in the newlywed stage of their marriage, where every chance they got, they were groping each other. Rex once commented on it. Arthur replied something about making babies.

Well, that wouldn't happen in public, so why did they have to touch and kiss all the time? Even when Rex had been in love, he hadn't participated in random public displays of affection very often.

Okay, well, he did more than he wanted to admit.

Or remember.

He didn't want to miss her, even though she haunted his every dream.

"How was it out there today?" Maren asked, leaning into Arthur, her hand resting on his chest.

"I didn't catch much," Arthur said, kissing her cheek. "How was your day?"

"Candice and I had fun. Went shopping and had lunch."

"Hey, babe," Timothy said as he jumped onto the dock. "Ready to relieve Xander from babysitting duties?"

"Mauve and Richie are already there." Candice patted her stomach. "I thought you could take me out to celebrate."

Timothy cocked his head. "For what reason?"

"The fact we don't have to go on vacation this

time to achieve expanding our little family." Candice smiled.

Timothy smacked his forehead.

The rest of the guys hooted. A few whistled.

Rex gave his best shout. Of course, he was happy for his friend. Timothy wanted a big family. It's all he talked about. "Congratulations, man."

"We're going to the Waterway for dinner. Would you both like to join us? The whole crew is welcome." Maren always had a sweet smile and a kind voice. She never left anyone out and always made him feel welcome, even when he was the odd man out.

Rex could understand how any man would be mesmerized by Maren's unique look with her tanned complexion, dark, inviting eyes, warm smile, and gentle personality. Deep down, Rex knew not all women were like his mother.

Or his ex.

Candice leaned into her husband. "I think we'll pass tonight."

"What about you, Rex? Will you join us?" Maren asked.

"Thanks, but I will cook up the fish we caught today. You've got to eat it while it's fresh," Rex said.

"Everyone except Hawke, who has a hot date, was planning on hanging on the boat with me."

Maren pursed her lips, looking sad and disappointed. She didn't feel sorry for him, but she'd once told him she sensed an emptiness in him that could only have been created by heartache. He'd laughed it off, even though he knew Maren was perceptive and dead-on right.

She was always right.

Rex glanced toward the shore and his breath hitched, catching the beauty he'd never forgotten. He lowered his sunglasses, peering over the rim. "No fucking way."

A tall, slender woman with long blond hair bouncing over her shoulders like in a shampoo commercial strolled across the parking lot wearing what could only be described as pink fuck-me pumps and a floral dress that hugged her body like a second skin. She sported big white sunglasses, and her plump, glossy lips attracted a ray of sunshine, lighting up her sultry face. She looked like an actress or model promenading across the red carpet.

And reminded him of everything in his past.

And everything he thought his future would hold.

"Whoa. Who is that?" Maren asked.

"Tilly Bettencourt." The name rolled off his tongue, triggering a kaleidoscope of memories swirling in his mind, sending heat to all the wrong places.

"You know her?" Arthur asked.

"Yeah," he said with a dry, scratchy throat.

"And? Who is she to you?" Timothy asked.

"My ex-girlfriend or my stepsister, depending on how you want to spin it." Rex ranked his hand through his hair. His heart dropped to his toes. "Unfuckingbelievable," he muttered. This was about the lowest of all the low-down dirty things his mother could do to get him to come home.

"That requires some explaining," Kent said.

"It will have to wait." Rex rubbed the back of his neck. "I know I promised all of you some grilled fish, but I need to talk with her alone and knowing her, she's not going away quietly."

"Is that your way of telling us to fuck off?" Duncan asked.

"Something like that," Rex said. "I'll text you all later."

"If you need backup, you know how to reach us." Buddy jumped onto the dock. The rest of the men followed, and the entire crew eased on toward the marina. To their credit, they didn't eye the approaching storm coming his way and just kept walking.

He sucked in his breath and mentally prepared himself for the wrath he knew was coming.

When Tilly Bettencourt had been given Rex's address, she expected a top-notch yacht club, not your average joe marina, where she had to assume he had the most excellent, most expensive boat in all the marina. She paused at the end of the dock for a second, staring at a bare-chested Rex on the back of what she guessed to be at least a fifty-foot Absolute. Nice boat, but a little small and not quite right for a man worth close to forty-two million dollars.

Of course, Rex wanted to pretend he didn't come from money. He'd always had a hard time accepting the idea that he could do whatever he wanted, whenever he wanted, which is why she totally understood his career choice.

Her body shivered, remembering how his fingers dug into her ass and how his lips sizzled against her skin. How he'd whispered sweet, loving words into her ear every chance he got. He'd been an attentive boyfriend. If they went out on a date, he paid attention to her and nothing else mattered. He was never on his phone. He never wanted to be out with his buddies instead. He was kind and considerate, and she hated to admit it, but she missed him each and every day.

No one she'd met could ever hold a candle to Rex.

She sucked in a deep breath, the salty air burning her lungs as she stepped with wobbly legs onto the dock. Wearing three-inch heels had been a dumb idea, but Rex had always loved it when she wore sexy shoes and formfitting clothes. He worshipped her body and admired her brains.

At one time, he loved her.

And she still loved him.

He lowered his head, looking over his designer sunglasses, mouth gaping open.

At least she still affected him ten years later. Though she wasn't exactly sure if he was gawking or glaring. Either way, she figured he wouldn't be too happy she'd just shown up. The last time she'd seen him, he'd mentioned that living in a dumpster would be better than ever having to lay eyes on her again.

She did her best to ignore the group of people that had exited his yacht as they passed.

The closer she got to the boat, the slower she walked. She breathed slowly, trying to calm her racing pulse. Clutching her purse, she hoped her trembling hands didn't give away her lack of confidence. She hated being vulnerable, but she'd made a promise.

If anything, she was as good as her word.

"Hello, Rex," she said, lifting her sunglasses up, letting them rest on the top of her head, keeping her recently styled hair from falling in her face.

"What are you doing here?" He planted his hands on his hips, just over his low-hanging shorts. On his chest, he'd gotten a tattoo of some kind of compass with fire around it.

She tilted her head, searching the side of his arm for the tattoo he'd gotten when they'd been dating. He must have sensed what she was searching for as he twisted his body, giving her a bird's-eye view of the two hearts she'd doodled on her notebooks in high school with the words: *2 hearts 1 love.*

Heat burned her cheeks.

"I've come to talk some sense into you," she said.

"You came on your own? Or did someone send

you?" His accusatory tone smacked her skin like large water pellets slamming to the ground.

"Does it matter?"

"It always matters." Rex stepped back, ducking his head into a cooler. He lifted a beer, twisting the top and chugging half.

"You're not going to invite me aboard?" She put one hand on her hip.

"Nope. And I'm not going home either, so you can tell my mother I got the message."

"You're being a childish asshole."

Tilly took a deep, calming breath. "Help me on the yacht," she said.

"Not with those shoes. You'll either tear the leather seats or break your neck."

"Fine," she said, leaning over, pulling one shoe off, then the other. Tucking her purse under her armpit, she dangled the shoes from one hand, holding out the other.

"I still don't want you on my boat." He took a long draw from his beer, eyeing her with his golden eyes. "Go home, Tilly. Tell my mother whatever you want, but I'm not rushing to her bedside."

"Your mother didn't send me." She tossed her shoes and purse on the boat and stretched out her hand.

He just stood there.

"Jerk," she mumbled before grabbing the railing and climbing aboard. "Your father did."

He gagged on his beer, spewing the liquid down his chest and onto the deck.

She breezed past him, lifting the lid on the outside cooler and grabbing a cold one for herself. Her entire life, she'd been called a contradiction. Raised a socialite, she had a flare for the finer things in life, like her three-hundred-dollar shoes on the luxury cruiser's back bench. Her closet was filled with designer clothes, much like the one-of-a-kind dress she had on, which was created by an up-and-coming designer.

Tilly might have been homecoming queen and dabbled in modeling during high school, but she'd also been captain of her volleyball team, which got her a college scholarship to the same school Rex had been recruited to play golf. She'd never been afraid of hard work, and upon graduating, a year after Rex had walked out of her life, she volunteered for the Peace Corps, spending over three years as a health advisor in a remote village in South America. She had survived living on about a dollar a day, with no running water and no air-conditioning. Her bathroom was a shared outhouse, and she had to take bucket baths.

She continued to work for the Peace Corps in the recruitment office and occasionally took short assignments when needed.

Holding out the beer, she waited for Rex to take it and be the gentleman she knew he could be. But when he just stared at her, she shrugged her shoulders and easily twisted off the top. She'd developed a taste for beer in college, and it had never left her, but it always reminded her of the only man she would ever love.

"My father asked you to come? Why would he do that?"

"Because he's not a selfish prick, like his son."

"Swearing isn't becoming of a lady." Rex snagged another beer before plopping himself down on the back bench.

She laughed. "I'm not a docile little lady, and you used to think it was cute when I uttered the unexpected obscenity."

"I'd be lying if you weren't still, well… drop-dead gorgeous, but that doesn't change the past." He stretched out his legs, resting his feet on the cushion. "I'll call my dad later and tell him you came, asked me to come home, and that I said no."

"What is wrong with you?" She sat down on the chair across from him. The cruiser was more of a home than a yacht, so it wasn't surprising that Rex had opted to live on it. He had always had a thing for the water. "Your mother is dying, and all she wants is to see her youngest before she goes. Your sister misses you. Your brother is a dad now and would love to have you meet your nephew. I don't think that is too much to ask for you to return, to give a dying woman some peace, regardless of the past."

"You called me selfish. Well, I must get that from my mother since all she thinks about is herself." He didn't look in her direction, keeping his head turned, facing the Intracoastal. He waved to a boat that eased by.

"I didn't expect you to come home three years ago when my dad passed away unexpectedly, but Louisa is your mother, and she's been heartbroken ever since you left."

Rex laughed. "So heartbroken she couldn't tear herself away from her lover to save her family." Every syllable was laced with the same angry tone he had the day he'd found out about the affair.

"My parents were separated, and you chose to

ignore the fact that your parents fought all the time and barely shared the same bed anymore."

He snapped his attention to her, ripping off his sunglasses. "You didn't come home and find your mother sucking face with the man you expected to be your father-in-law, not your stepfather."

"I can't believe we're having this same argument. What's worse is that you've held on to this all these years. Your father and siblings have forgiven her. They are at your mother's bedside every day. Your father, and even his wife, Judy, were there for your mother when my dad died. If you had stuck around long enough to work through what happened, you'd see how much better off everyone was."

"That's fucked up," he said, dropping his feet to the floor and leaning forward. "My mother didn't come to my matches because she was too busy screwing your dad. Your dad didn't go to your games because he was holed up in some hotel with my mother. Have you forgotten those betrayals? Forgotten that their affair had been going on for years?" He stood and closed the gap, lifting her out of her chair, holding her gaze with fire in his honey eyes. "In the last ten years, I've heard from my mother only a handful of times, and each time all she'd cared about was explaining why it happened and how happy she'd finally been with your dad. She didn't once care about me or how I felt. Only that I'd accept what she'd done and act as if it were the best thing since sliced bread."

She swallowed. His fingers curled around her arms, burning their imprint into her skin like a cattle prod. They'd all been angry and upset when the truth came out. Tilly had told her father that she hated him. She'd cried for hours, feeling humiliated. But the worst part was that her boyfriend couldn't, or wouldn't, give her any comfort.

He tilted his head, leaning in, a scant few inches from her face. Licking his lips, he moved in for the kill, pressing his warm lips over hers, teasing her with his tongue.

Her body stiffened for a moment before turning into putty. Her chest rose, compressing her breasts against his hard body. Ten years ago, he'd been her world. Her rock. The only person who truly understood her. She wrapped her arms around his broad shoulders.

He snapped his head back, breaking off the tumultuous kiss. "My mother made her choice, and it wasn't her family."

"And you made yours, and it wasn't me."

He cocked his head, dropping his hands to his sides. "That's rich. I begged you to come with me."

"You ordered me, demanded I give up my education and never speak to my family again. I loved you, but I loved my family too. My sisters and brothers needed me. My mother needed me, and I needed you, but you"—she poked his chest—"acted like a spoiled brat, and when things didn't go your way, you took off." Her insides still shook from the earth-shattering kiss. Memories of their love affair collided with the pain he'd caused his entire family when he'd cut off all communication, blocking phone numbers, going dark on the internet, making himself a ghost.

But mostly, how he'd punctured her heart, leaving it with a gaping hole that, no matter what she tried, she'd never been able to fill the space he left behind.

His eyes narrowed to tiny slits. "Joining the Air Force, becoming a firefighter, and now working with the Aegis Network have been the best things that ever happened to me. I have no regrets."

"Neither do I." She swallowed the guttural sob that lodged in her throat.

"Good. Now get off my boat and go home."

She folded her arms, sitting back down. "I'm

not going anywhere until you agree to come back with me."

"When hell freezes over," he said.

Dark clouds rolled in off the ocean. The smell of salty rain filled the humid air that clung to her skin.

"I can wait," she said defiantly.

"Suit yourself." He stepped into the galley, closing the door.

She heard the click of the lock.

It was going to be a long night.

The wind howled as it brought the first few raindrops that pelted the fiberglass yacht. It never rained long in Florida during the summer months, but when it did, it came down hard, fast, and with loud claps of thunder. The cruiser rocked with the waves of the Intracoastal Waterways.

Rex lay on the king-size bed that took up most of the single bedroom, staring up at the portal on the boat's bow. His stomach growled, but he didn't feel like getting out of bed. It had been over an hour since he'd left Tilly sitting on the deck. He assumed she was long gone by now, considering the coming storm. He ran his fingers across his lips. Kissing her had been stupid, and he had no idea why he'd done it other than he wanted to know if she still tasted like honey.

Which she did.

He blinked, pulling up an image of his mother when he'd been a small boy. Her dark hair touched her shoulders. He had his mother's whiskey-colored eyes. When he was a kid, he thought his mother was the most beautiful woman ever, always full of life. He couldn't imagine what battling stage-four ovarian cancer was doing to her body.

The evening sky lit up with multiple lightning strikes. Thunder pounded as the rain came down in a continuous stream.

"Rex! Let me in, please."

He sprang from the bed, racing from the room through the main cabin, eating area, and the galley, finally reaching the door. He unlocked the latch. "What the hell are you still doing here?" He stepped back, helping a drenched Tilly down the steps.

"Waiting for hell to freeze over."

"Didn't you see the storm coming?"

She nodded. "I thought you'd let me in when it started to rain."

"I thought you'd leave," he said, holding up his hand. "Stay there. I'll get you a towel."

He left her standing at the threshold, looking like a drowned rat. He should have known. The woman rarely took no for an answer. She had to be one of the most stubborn, pigheaded women he'd ever met. Glancing out the window, he searched for a break in the clouds, but all he found was more darkness.

After getting a towel, he ducked into his room and snagged a pair of shorts and a T-shirt. She'd swim in them, but it was better than the wet dress she currently had on.

"You can change into these." He tossed her the towel and the clothes, ensuring he kept a safe distance. His heart pounded against his chest, reminding him of how she'd destroyed it.

"Thank you," she said, ruffling her tangled blond locks with the towel as she breezed by, leaving a scented trail of honey and fresh pineapple. She'd been the hottest and most popular girl in high school, and it wasn't because she was rich.

It was because she was as sweet as home-baked cookies and had a big heart. He'd known her his entire life, having grown up at the same country club. As children, they took swimming lessons and played paddle tennis against one another. For the majority of their lives, they'd been friends. Not close friends, since they didn't really hang out together outside of the club, but close enough.

His stomach rumbled. "Tilly, have you eaten dinner?" he yelled toward the bedroom.

"No, but I wouldn't want you to go to any trouble. I mean, you would have let me drown."

He chuckled. "Trust me, I'm not bending over backward for you. But I have to eat." He told himself he'd feed her while they waited for the storm to pass, and then he'd send her packing. He'd just have to make her understand there was nothing left for him at home.

He pulled out all the ingredients he needed to make a pan-seared grouper with asparagus, which she hated and that made him smile. God, he was an asshole. He took the knife and started chopping the garlic when she stepped into the galley wearing his T-shirt and shorts. They hid her perfect body with their bagginess, but she was still the sexiest woman on the planet.

Razor-sharp pain tinged his finger.

"Fuck," he muttered, dropping the knife. He stared at his hand. A few drops of blood trickled from his index finger.

"Let me do that. You always put too much garlic in anyway." She moved him to the side with her warm, sexy hands. Memories of them roaming his body pelted his brain.

He should have been a real prick and not let her in. He cleaned up his wound, put a Band-Aid on it, and heated up the skillet.

She stood next to him, slicing and dicing before reaching across him and dumping the onions, garlic, and other seasonings in the pan with a dash of olive oil. Her hair brushed his shoulder. In college, when they had lived together, they enjoyed cooking together. They moved in the kitchen, much like synchronized swimmers cutting through the water with precision.

"I'll finish up. Why don't you go sit down at the table?" He needed to put some distance between their bodies and clear the teenage hormones from his mind. Over the years, he'd run through various potential conversations he might have with her, none of which included cooking fish together.

"Do you have any white wine?" she asked.

"There's a bottle open in the fridge and more in the cooler." Wine was a mistake, and he knew it, but he decided to check his prick personality at the door and enjoy a good meal. "Glasses are in that cabinet to the right of the sink."

A loud clap of thunder boomed through the

night as more lightning brightened the inside of the boat.

"I love a good thunderstorm," she said, placing a wineglass next to the stove.

He ignored the tightening in his muscles and the tingling sensation crawling across his fingertips, itching to dig into her soft curves. The fish sizzled as he flipped it. He focused on his growling stomach and sipped his wine, not wanting to go sit at the table and continue to pretend this wasn't the most awkward situation either one of them had ever been in.

"My father really asked you to come?"

"He said you hadn't returned his phone calls, except for a few random text messages that work was too hectic for you to get away."

He placed a plate of food before her and joined her at the table.

"Imagine my surprise when I get here and find out you're on a few days' vacation from the fire station and have no assignments with the Aegis Network for at least a week." She looked to the ceiling, pressing her forefinger to her temple. "And today was the first day."

"Spying on me?"

She shook her head, letting out a sarcastic

laugh. "I called the station when I landed. It took being transferred to a few different people before I was informed about both situations."

"You're lucky I'm still here. But you still wasted your time."

"I had to try," she said, lowering her gaze. "Your mom is in bad shape."

"My dad texted me yesterday and said Mom had maybe a month left and that at this point, she refused all treatment except for pain medication." He gulped his wine. He'd actually bought a plane ticket to go back to Kent Island, Maryland, leaving tomorrow morning at seven, but he'd decided not to go. It wasn't just that he had struggled to forgive his mother or that he'd become estranged from his siblings and father, but there were certain things he couldn't get out of his mind.

No one could deny how much he'd been hurt or what it had done to see his mother adjusting her clothing as she and Mr. Bettencourt stepped from the master bedroom. Rex might have been an adult, but that would fuck up any young man.

"It's not just your mom who wants to see you," Tilly said.

Rex picked at the food on his plate. The first few years after he'd left home had been fueled by anger. He dealt with it by becoming the best fire protection specialist the Air Force had ever seen and ignored his past, including his money, but then he wanted this yacht after he'd left the military, so he tapped into his trust fund and that's what triggered an onslaught of messages from his father.

His sister, Emily, had sent him a nasty gram a few years ago, telling him to get his head out of his ass. His brother constantly sent him pictures of family gatherings. He knew more about them than they did about him.

Not that there was anything to know. He worked. He fished. He worked.

"I don't know about that. My little correspondence with Emily and Miles has been tainted with resentment." A sentiment he understood and had held on to for years. They hadn't been the ones to catch their mother nor the ones who had to break the news to their father, but they both seemed to blame Rex. Not for the breakup of their parents' marriage but for hurting their mother.

He chugged his wine before pouring another hearty glass.

"I'd go easy on that."

"I'd mind your own business," he said, wishing he could take back the harsh tone.

She leaned back, folding her arms under her breasts.

This was so not the right time to consider her naked body under his T-shirt, though it was a very nice distraction from pondering if he should grant his mother her dying wish or hold on to anger for the rest of his life. He'd wrapped himself in a bubble of resentment, which protected his heart but walled him off from having any meaningful relationships, even with his brothers-in-arms.

He swallowed that revelation.

"You're a piece of work," she said, shaking her head. "All you have to do is show up, say hello, and then you can go back to hiding out on your boat, pretending you have a life, when really, all you have is a lot of nothing."

"You know jack shit about my life," he said with a snarl. "I have a great career and fantastic friends. Friends who won't fuck me over like my own family. Or my girlfriend."

"Seriously? You're going to sit there and tell me I screwed you over? Do you hear yourself? You're so goddamn angry over something that happened ten years ago. You've never moved past it. No. You've chosen to make it the bane of your existence."

"Tilly, you don't have a fucking clue about my life."

"Please. You live on a boat."

"What does that have to do with anything?" He took his glass and stood, leaning against the counter. "I love this yacht. I love being on the water, and you know that."

"All right. Then tell me why you left the military. You weren't in all that long. Seems like you're jumping from one thing to the next. That doesn't sound like a happy, content person to me."

He turned, lifting up his shirt, showing off a few of his scars. "One really bad mission that went sideways was enough for me and my team to decide there were other ways to serve." He tugged at the fabric. "That group of men you passed on the dock. We were all fire protection specialists in the Air Force together. A buddy of ours offered us a job with the Aegis Network while we were recovering from various injuries. We all looked at each other and decided as a group to leave. We all now work at the same station and for Aegis. We're a family." He cocked a brow. "So don't go telling me shit about my life when you haven't a clue."

She sat up a little taller. "That's fair, but you also don't know what your family or the rest of us have

been through. While you're out here doing whatever, they have been suffering. Would it be so
fucking difficult to get on a plane, go to Maryland,
and spend one day with a dying woman? Not everything has to be about you. Or even the past. No one
is asking you to cut off your damn arm or to
swallow your pride. Just spend a little time with your
blood. After that, you can return to your awesome
life and forget about the rest of us. Again."

He slowly sipped his wine. Her words chipped
at his anger. He'd held on to it like a badge of
honor. How would he ever know if he could get
over it if he never returned? "All right, you win. I'll
go home."

Tilly fluffed the pillow Rex had given her and tried
to get comfortable on the sofa. She had no idea why
she'd insisted on taking the couch when he'd offered
her a nice, plush king-size bed, but she was brutally
stubborn.

A trait that got her in trouble.

Often.

The first year he'd been gone, she tracked his
whereabouts and booked airline tickets to see him

half a dozen times. But every time she got to the airport, her stubbornness prevented her from taking the trip. She cringed, remembering the amount of money she'd spent that year all because she thought *he* should be the one to come to her since he'd called things off.

She pulled the soft 600-thread-count sheets to her chin. The wind and rain had died down, but the boat rocked gently in the water. She'd had a crush on Rex for as long as she could remember. At school, he barely gave her the time of day, but she had his full attention at the club, except when he was on the golf course. The first time he'd made the cut for the club championship, at the ripe old age of fifteen, she'd offered to be his caddy. The only time she ever golfed had been with him. He'd always told her she should take up the game, but it was only fun if she played with him.

It wasn't until after he'd won the club championship that year that she told him she liked him as more than a friend.

She smiled, remembering the stunned look on his face after she'd kissed him. He'd blinked a half dozen times and opened and closed his mouth a dozen more until he wrapped his arms around her and bruised her lips with a burning kiss.

Those days were long gone, and they were both very different people.

The light from his room seeped out into the main cabin. "This is ridiculous. That sofa is the most uncomfortable thing in the world. It's the only thing about this boat that sucks."

"I'm not going to ask you to give up your bed. Besides, I lived in a third-world country on a foam bed topper for three years. This is like the Ritz, comparatively."

"You did what?" He stepped into the room wearing nothing but boxers and muscles. Damn. He'd always been a fine specimen of a man, and the thirty-two-year-old version wasn't any different.

"You didn't know I was in the Peace Corps after college?"

"No, but I was either in basic training, fire school, or deployed for the first four years after I left. I did hear you worked for the Peace Corps, though. I just figured it was in the office. You were always good at managing things that helped people." He scratched the back of his head.

"How on earth did you know I worked for the Peace Corps, but not know I was a volunteer and lived in South America for three years."

"In one of my sister's random emails where she

berates me for not coming home, she mentioned something about your career."

Wow. He'd really gotten over her.

Quickly.

Of course, she dealt with her grief over their breakup by disconnecting as much as possible.

But it hadn't helped to erase her love for him.

"South America? I spent some time there in the military. We came in contact with some Peace Corps Volunteers," he said. "Some of them lived in incredibly remote areas. I'm struggling with Little Miss Designer Everything doing that."

"Well, believe it. I did it. And I survived." She smiled.

"Come on." Standing at the side of the sofa, he held out a hand.

"I'm not kicking you out of your room."

"It's a king-size bed. We've slept in smaller."

She raised a brow as her heart hammered in her chest. "I'm not going to sleep with you."

"Yeah, you are. And the key word is sleep. Not sex. We used to sleep in that double bed we had all the time and not have sex."

"We'd wake up and have sex."

"That's true." He leaned over, taking her by the hand. "But I won't be able to sleep knowing you're out here on this. I can promise I won't even think about sex, much less touch you."

"That's exactly what every woman wants to hear when a man is wooing her to bed." She stood, sliding her hands from his, snagging the pillow.

He raised his arms. "I'm trying to be nice and respectful here, but I also want to make sure we both get some sleep."

"I get the right side," she said. Good grief, what the hell was she doing agreeing to share his bed? Did she have some sadomasochistic tendencies she didn't know about?

Or had she just lost her mind?

"You're still particular about that?"

"Aren't you?" She held the hem of his shirt down, making sure it covered her ass. She should have kept his shorts on.

"About what side I sleep on? God, no. Then again, I generally don't have women in my bed so what difference does it make."

She stopped at the doorway.

"Umph." He bumped into her.

"Generally? What does that mean?"

He pressed his hand into the small of her back, nudging her forward. "It means I'm not seeing anyone and haven't in a while and don't like women on my boat. Cramps my style. Now stop talking and get into bed before I change my mind."

That statement sent her insides on a roller-coaster ride. The downhill turns were filled with jealousy over any woman who'd had him after her. The uphill twists were all about the fact he hadn't been with anyone in a while.

The only question was, what constituted a while, and did he stay at their places instead?

She mentally smacked herself as she pulled back the sheets and slipped onto the soft but firm mattress.

The bed shifted as he sat down, his back to her. The pitter-patter of light raindrops echoed off the boat. As he twisted, the outside light gleamed through the porthole like a ray of sunshine on the heart tattoo. Without thinking, she reached out and traced the letters inside the heart. "I can't believe you didn't change this."

He rolled to his side, propping himself on his elbow. "I honestly never thought to change it. Besides, I like it."

"Your father was so pissed when you got that." Mindlessly, she continued to run her fingers on his shoulders.

"I remember being upset with you for not getting a matching one."

"Back then, it scared me too much."

"Does that mean you have one now?"

"I've got a couple of them," she admitted, jerking her hand away. "We should get some sleep." As if she could relax enough to doze even for a short period. As soon as he drifted off, she planned on sneaking out, which was stupid. She didn't have to stay in his bed, and she certainly didn't care if he thought her rude for not taking him up on his chivalrous act.

"Where?" he asked, rolling to his back.

"Back of my neck and lower back."

"Of what?"

She tucked her hands under her cheek and closed her eyes. "On my lower back is a set of butterflies."

"You always did love those insects." His chest rose and fell in a rhythmic pattern. "And the other one?"

"It's late. I'm tired." No way. She didn't dare to tell him. And it didn't matter.

"Come on, just tell me."

She squeezed her eyes closed and let out a long sigh. "The same one you have on your biceps."

"Are you serious?" Rex bolted upright, ripping the covers from their bodies. He reached across her and flicked on the reading lamp. "You've got this on your neck?" He tapped the tattoo he'd gotten right before they graduated from high school. The intention had been that they would both get the tattoo, but after watching the needles dig into his arm, Tilly had chickened out. He couldn't blame her. It did hurt, and the smell of burning flesh was an acquired taste. "When?"

"About seven years ago." She sat up and rubbed the back of her neck, her hair flowing over her shoulders. "I'd finished my initial service for the Peace Corps and extended my stay. I went home for a week for a family wedding, and I found a box of stuff from high school. The drawing we took to the guy who did yours was there, and I remembered my promise. So, I got it."

He ignored the fact that the wedding she referred to had been his mother's to her father, a thought that still weirded him out on so many levels. "Can I see it?" His pulse raced faster than the first time he'd run into a burning building. Of course, the second he'd crossed the threshold, he didn't notice his heartbeat, and his training kicked in.

No one had ever trained him on how to deal with an ex-girlfriend who fulfilled a promise long after the relationship ended, never telling him about it either.

She turned, raising her hair up, exposing the back of her neck and a matching tattoo.

"Why? Why did you do that?" He reached out with a shaky hand, his index finger hovering over the letters. He recoiled when she let her hair fall. The wavy locks bounced over her shoulders.

"I don't know. Maybe in a weird way, I thought I owed it to you. Or maybe it was closure."

He pushed her hair to the side, unmasking the symbol that once represented their undying love.

He inched closer, studying the design. "This is a little different than mine."

"No, it's not." She tried to turn, but he grabbed her arms, holding her steady.

"What's this?" He followed the lines—there were letters etched in the lining of one of the hearts—*R K J.* "My initials?" His throat dropped to his stomach. A woman didn't permanently scar her skin with a man's name when she was looking for closure.

She cleared her throat, smoothing down her hair as she scooted to the edge of the bed. "I was feeling sentimental."

"Seriously? You tattooed my initials into your neck over an emotional moment about the past?"

She sprang from the bed, her head hitting the low ceiling.

"Shit," she whispered, sitting back down.

"Are you okay?" He palmed her shoulder, his fingers tangling in her soft hair.

"My head is fine, but I'm not." She shrugged his arm off. "It wasn't an emotional moment, as you called it. You're a huge part of my past, and I wanted something from that time. My dad and your mom had just gotten married and—"

"And their union made you want to engrave me on your neck?"

"I'm sorry this is freaking you out."

"I'm not the one who just leaped from the bed." He patted the mattress. "I am, however, very curious." He was more than curious. He was utterly fascinated, not to mention it inflated his bruised ego when it came to how easily Tilly let him walk away. For the first time in ten years, he felt connected to the past that had ultimately betrayed him in the worst way.

"I never had any intention of telling you." She pulled her hair to the side, twirling it in her hands as she leaned back against the headboard. "I thought if I got the tattoo, I would be able to prove to myself that I was finally over you leaving me. The initials I had done a year later when I got the butterflies."

"So, I was an afterthought," he mumbled, unsure of the sensations swirling in his gut. He positioned himself next to her, their arms touching ever so slightly, but enough that it generated the kind of raw heat that reminded him she was every bit a woman.

"I wouldn't say an afterthought, exactly. I really

don't know how to explain it all without sounding like a crazy, psycho ex-girlfriend."

"Yeah, it's a little nuts." His thoughts bounced through his past like a rubber ball from one memory to the next, landing on the last time he saw her and the utter pain it had put in his soul. He didn't deny that she felt it too. He never had. But she chose everything but him and that hurt more than what his mother had done.

"Trust me, I know. But getting over you dumping me was the hardest thing I've ever had to do."

"Harder than living in a third-world country?" he asked. Dumbass question, but the mood was too intense, and he needed a little lightness to get through it. "And I need to clear up one thing. I didn't dump you."

"Oh my God. Yes, you did. Why can't you admit it? Sometimes you are most definitely more stubborn than I am."

"That's impossible and I'll agree that we both called it quits." Everything she'd ever meant to him came crashing down on his heart, squeezing his life out. For years, he'd been telling himself that he didn't need or even want her. But the ugly truth was he'd never gotten over the fact that she'd never chased after him. Never called him or looked for him. A childish thing to hold on to, but it still hurt as much as how his mother scolded him for telling his father what he'd seen before she got a chance to do it herself. His mother made it clear it was her life and he had no right butting in.

Only it affected everything he'd done from that day forward.

Now, to find out, Tilly had done the one thing she couldn't do when they were together, years after they broke up. While a sweet gesture, it was odd, especially when he believed her life had gone on without her ever thinking twice about him or what they could have been.

He also no longer knew what to think about his inability to call her over the years. Not once did he ever think that she, or his mother for that matter, was hurting like he had been. His mother's letters, while she begged for his forgiveness and told him how much she missed him, were all about how happy she was. How happy the whole family was.

Without him.

That was the underlying message and it was a hard pill to swallow.

"You didn't give us a chance," she said. Her

dark-blue eyes captured his gaze, holding him hostage.

"You told me if I left, we were done."

"Only after you said that if I loved you, I'd drop out of college and run off with you, turning my back on my family."

He lay down, resting his head on her thighs, looking up at her. "You were always a stubborn mule."

"I still am," she said, smiling, running her fingers through his hair. "But so were you."

"Tell me something. Did you wear those heels and dress to get me all hot and bothered so you could get me to do what you wanted?"

"What do you think?"

"You could make a pair of ratty old gym shorts look sexy." He reached up, cupping the back of her neck, rolling his thumb in a tiny circle just behind her earlobe, drawing her plump, luscious lips closer to his.

"What are you doing?"

"I'm getting ready to kiss you."

"You promised you'd keep your hands to yourself." Her pink tongue darted out, rolling across her mouth in an exotic ritual.

He lifted his head, getting lost in her sea-blue eyes. "I can roll over right now and go to sleep, or I can do something as crazy as tattooing your initials on my arm."

Her hot breath covered his face in a warm blanket. "Us being together isn't a good idea."

"I know. But it seems like we both need something so we can move forward."

She arched a brow. "Are you suggesting we have one last romp in the sack as a way to get some sort of resolution to the way we ended things ten years ago?"

"Either that, or I could go get TAB tattooed in my hearts."

"You could, but you won't."

"You know how I appreciate a good dare," he said, enjoying how easily they fell into their old banter, like the ten years was more like ten days. "How about we stop talking." He took her mouth in a tender, deep, passionate kiss, probing every succulent crevice.

Her hands glided across his chest as she sprawled out next to him. Their lovemaking had always been filled with a combination of delicate compassion and a raw craving that left them breathless. Not a single woman since had satisfied his appetite the way she had. Sure, he'd had some great sex with some really hot women, but they didn't make his blood turn to smoldering lava.

His hands roamed her body, feeling every soft curve. All he wanted was to feel her warm skin against his. Lifting her shirt up, he ducked his head into the crevice of her neck, kissing and nibbling on her earlobe. He palmed her breast, enjoying her soft moans.

His body told him to devour every inch of her.

His brain whispered to stop.

His heart begged him to stand up and go sleep on the extremely uncomfortable sofa.

He jerked his head back, staring down at her.

"What's wrong?" she asked.

"Nothing." He cupped her chin with his thumb and forefinger, ignoring his heart. She couldn't hurt him anymore. They weren't destined to be together, and after this trip home to give closure to his mother, Tilly would walk out of his life again.

No. He'd walk out of hers.

Slipping his hand into her cotton panties, he cupped her smooth, bare sex, circling his fingers over her hard nub.

She arched her back, raising her breasts to his

mouth. Her hips rolled slowly against his palm. He remembered every inch of her body and knew exactly what it craved. He teased her, nibbling on her nipples, slowly sliding his finger in and out. She tried to get him to increase the speed and pressure, but he kept his strokes deliberate and soft.

Teasing her to the brink of begging had always been a pleasure he'd never quite been able to capture again.

In one swift motion, he yanked her underwear to her ankles, tossing them across the room. He stared at her shaven womanhood that glistened with desire. Cupping both her breasts, he bent over, first breathing on her before licking gently.

She clutched his head, pushing him against her.

"Please, don't torture me. I can't take it."

"But it's half the fun." He pulled back just enough to continue brushing his lips and tongue gently across her soft sex. She smelled like bottled sunshine and tasted like a warm day on the beach with a tinge of salt in the air.

Her fingers dug into his scalp as she arched her back, raising her hips higher.

He pinched and twisted her nipples, enjoying her deep throaty groans.

"Jesus, would you just do it," she said in a pant.

He smiled against her, clamping his mouth over her, sucking on her hard nub until she dug her ankles into his back. Her body jerked and thrashed about the bed, legs squeezing his head, and her creamy climax spilled out, coating his mouth and fingers, igniting a deep burn across his skin.

He had to have her. Right now. He couldn't wait.

He kissed the inside of her thigh, making his way down her long, silky legs. Standing, he removed his shorts and found a condom. He held the foil wrapper up to his mouth, preparing to tear it with his teeth.

She'd propped up on her elbows, knees bent, staring at him with a mischievous smile. "You know what I want now."

"Seriously? You still have to do that? Every time you have sex?"

She cocked her head. "Don't all women?"

He wished. "Not the ones I've met."

"Well, sex shouldn't happen without it."

He tossed the condom on the bed. "Do with me what you want. I'm not going to complain."

"Never complain, only beg me to stop."

"Yeah, in about three seconds, unless you want this to end with oral."

"That would be a travesty," she whispered.

He sucked in a breath, gritting his teeth as she took him in her soft hands, gliding them up and down. Her tongue swirled over the top, taking just the tip into her mouth.

He hissed as she squeezed his shaft, cupping him, easing him into her mouth with her hot lips. He used to tease her about her insatiable appetite for giving blow jobs. The first one she'd ever given, he swore she had to be lying that she'd never done it before. The way she admired him as she toyed with him, bringing him the kind of pleasure that made a man weak at his knees.

He let out a long guttural groan, clenching his fists, doing his best not to grab her head and slam deep inside her mouth. Though he knew from past experience she wouldn't be opposed, that is not how he wanted this to end.

"You've got to stop," he ground out, swelling inside her, on the verge of losing all control.

She reached for the condom, tearing it open with her teeth.

"Christ, that is so hot," he said.

She smiled, rolling the barrier over his length. "So, your favorite or mine?"

"Yours." He might last a little longer that way,

saving himself some embarrassment of acting like a horny teenager who climaxed the second he was touched.

She raised up on her knees, wrapping her arms around his shoulders, pressing her lips against his. "Get on your back, Rex," she whispered. She'd never been afraid to express herself or ask for what she wanted, needed.

Who was he to deny her?

She straddled him, resting her sex against his. She rubbed her clit gently over him while she plucked at her nipples, biting her lower lip. Gliding one hand down her stomach, she flicked her fingers across herself, scraping her nails against his sensitive skin.

He grabbed her hips, moving them back and forth slightly, creating more friction where she needed it most. Biting down on the inside of his mouth, he held on to her so tight he worried he bruised her delicate skin. Her moans grew louder and her movements harder and faster until she rose up slightly, taking him inside.

He thrust his hips up, holding her over him for a long moment before repeating the motion. She tightened around him. "Yes," she said in a long moan, drenching him with her hot climax. She dropped her hands to his chest, her hair spilling over his face and body. "Rex," she whispered, grinding as he thrust inside her. He grunted as he flipped her on her back, ramming himself deep inside, burying his face in her neck as his body rippled with the kind of pleasure only she could give him.

He jerked, and his stomach twitched as he collapsed on top of her, their chests heaving up and down, breathless. He kissed her neck and earlobe.

Making love to her again didn't bring him closure. It only reminded him of why he loved her in the first place. It rattled his mind and opened the burning hole in his heart.

He rolled to the left because God forbid, she didn't have the right side of the bed and pulled the covers over their bodies. Holding her close, he did his best to push the slew of emotions back inside the little box he'd carried them in for all these years.

It was where they belonged and where he would need to keep them if he was ever going to get through this visit with his family. He wouldn't regret this. He couldn't.

He kissed her temple, snuggling up to her backside. He'd hold her all night. Like old times.

He'd allow himself this one little look into the past.

And then he'd sew up his heart and go on with his life.

4

R ex slipped from the bed, careful not to wake the sleeping beauty.

Quietly, he closed the bedroom door and made his way to the yacht's back deck. The morning sky gave way to the promise of the sun.

He glanced over his shoulder as if he could see Tilly tucked away in his bed.

The second he fought his first fire, he knew that's what he'd been born to do.

Just like loving Tilly.

He couldn't deny his feelings any more than he could ignore the guilt he tried to bury in some dark corner of his heart.

Deep down, he knew he'd return home to say goodbye to his mother. He had to, not just for her, but for him as well. The last few weeks the guilt had been eating him alive. It all came down to when it happened. His father had mentioned she had a month. But who could put a timetable on death and cancer.

No one.

Rex knew he had to do it sooner rather than later.

"Look, Daddy, it's Uncle Rex!" Elle Jordan waved from the edge of the dock.

"Shhh, quiet. People are still sleeping," Kent said.

"Hey, squirt. What are you two doing here so early?" Rex asked.

"Uncle Arthur said we could take his boat out and go fishing." Elle squared her shoulders and smiled proudly. "Oh, pretty shoes." Elle pointed to the pair of pink heels that Tilly had kicked off. "Do you have a girlfriend now? Does she have a friend she can introduce to my dad? He needs a girlfriend bad."

Rex covered his mouth, biting back his laughter.

"Elle, why don't you go start prepping the boat? I'll be right along." Kent jumped aboard while Elle skipped down the dock, swinging her arms back and forth.

"Out of the mouths of babes," Rex said.

"Yeah, but now I'm going to be fielding a million questions about what happened to the lady with the pink shoes." Kent shook his head. "Not to mention Elle just tried to fix me up with the school nurse."

"Oh my God. That's classic," Rex said. While it always proved difficult for Rex to be around small kids, he always enjoyed Elle and her spitfire personality. He respected Kent for his ability to raise a child alone since Elle's mother had died shortly after Elle had been born. Kent could have made other choices, but instead, he manned up and was the best father.

"So, care to tell me more about your visitor who opted to spend the night?" Kent asked. "I mean the whole stepsister thing needs some explaining."

"Technically, she is. But she was my girlfriend before my mom married her dad."

"That's just weird, so please don't ever tell Elle that. I would have no idea how to explain that one, and Elle has been asking so many questions lately about boys and girls and shit I'm not ready to discuss."

"That little girl is going to grow up on you." Rex slapped his buddy on the shoulder. "But not to worry. She won't cross Tilly's path. I'm flying home with her today to see my mom. She doesn't have much time left." Rex's throat was thick with emotion. The realization he would be coming face-to-face with his family under such intense circumstances sent his mind in a million directions.

"Wait. Tilly as in the one who created the tattoo on your shoulder? The girlfriend that—"

"Yep. That one." Rex didn't need to hear his buddy rattle off what little he'd shared about his life one night when he'd had too much to drink.

"And she spent the night?" Kent pointed to the cabin. "In there. With you?"

Rex wasn't the type to kiss and tell, but when he kept his mouth closed, he figured that spoke volumes.

Kent took a seat on the back bench. "You okay?"

Rex nodded, leaning against the console. "But I'll be honest, going home is freaking me right the fuck out. I've seen my father maybe five times in the last ten years. My brother about the same. My sister only twice, and my mom, well, not at all."

"I can't imagine going longer than a month without seeing my mom." Kent waved his hand toward Arthur's boat, where Elle was taking out all the fishing gear. "But all Elle has are a few pictures. She had only hours with her mother and obviously doesn't remember a thing. Only what I tell her and since I barely knew her mother, that's not much." Kent wiped his hand over his face. "I wish I had more stories to give her about her mom. And this phase she's going through about fixing me up with every woman she meets isn't really about me. It's about her wanting a mother."

"She's turning out just fine and you're an excellent father. I wouldn't worry about it."

Kent let out a long breath. "That's not the point. You've seen how she is with Maren and even my nanny Jackie. She's starved for female affection. I could be the best dad in all the land, but nothing can ever replace one's mother." Kent arched a brow. "Even in a boy's life."

"You are the best dad, and my situation is very different. My mother had a choice, and she chose to break up the family for her own selfish reasons."

"So, you chose to continue the madness and punish her. That, my friend, is damned selfish."

"Oh, what do you know," Rex said, waving his hand. "And it doesn't matter. I'm going to fulfill my mother's dying wish and go see her."

"Have you thought about what you'll say and how open you'll be to hearing your mom?"

"Not really." Was it too early to start drinking? Rex cracked his knuckles. To him, this wasn't about anything other than a quick visit. He'd see his family. He'd go through the motions. And then he'd leave.

Check.

Done.

"Do you know what you want from the visit?" Kent asked.

"Absolutely nothing." God, Rex loved Kent like a brother. He really did. But the man could be one big fucking pain in the ass when it came to *feelings*. "Except to fulfill an obligation."

"You're making a big mistake. This is an opportunity," Kent said. "How long have we known each other?"

"Since right after Elle was born." Rex waved to the precious little girl.

She smiled and waved right back.

"I know you don't like to talk about this shit, and other than a few drunken nights, you've kept it to yourself. But it's eating you alive, man." Kent leaned forward, resting his forearms on his knees. "Make peace with her. If you don't, you're going to regret it."

"She wants me to forgive, forget, and erase the past," Rex said. "My mother has this perception of what happened and can only see it from her eyes. She has always refused to see it from mine. How can she expect me to forgive her when she can't see what her choices did to me and everyone else?"

"Don't go getting all pissed off." Kent held up his hand. "But maybe you only see this through your truth and not anyone else's. I'm not saying what happened wasn't shitty. And of course, your mother could have made more appropriate choices before having an affair. But her marriage isn't any business of her children."

Rex cocked his head. "Does that mean any woman you date doesn't directly affect Elle?"

"Of course it does. She's not an adult. There's a big difference," Kent said. "We all know I don't date much because Elle's needs are more important to me than my sex life." He waggled his finger. "But that doesn't mean I don't have one. Or don't want a girlfriend. And if I ever found the right woman, it would be a dance. Elle would probably like her right away and then hate her guts until she loved her. It's how these things work. My point is you were put in a shitty situation. You were hurt and angry. But that was a long time ago. It's time to make it right before you no longer can."

Rex nodded.

"Daddy!" Elle called. "The boat's all ready."

"Time for me to go," Kent said. "If you need another one of my amazing pep talks, you know how to reach me."

"Enjoy your day." Rex watched as Elle greeted her dad with big wide-open arms and a kiss.

Their relationship was pretty incredible, even if Kent was worse than a paranoid mother and his dating life was actually nonexistent.

Tilly smoothed down the front of her dress and sucked in a deep breath. She should have thought about what the morning after would have been like, especially when she woke up alone in *his* bed.

"Are you ready?" he called from the deck, his suitcase in hand. "The traffic on ninety-five is going to be a bitch."

She took his hand, climbing the steps in the same dress she'd shown up in. All she could hope for was that none of his friends would bear witness to her walk of shame. She chomped down on her lower lip. Since when did she care what anyone but her family thought?

"Mind if I drive your rental?" he asked.

"That depends." She slipped her feet into her pumps and followed him down the dock. The sun shone bright in the morning sky as a few pelicans made their perch for the day on the tall dock posts. "Do you still drive like an old lady?" she asked, trying to ease the tension.

"I never drove slow, but you tended to drive like a racecar driver. Not to mention, you were the queen of tailgating."

She snagged the keys to the mid-size sedan from her purse, tossing them to him. "I hate Florida drivers, so you can drive."

Slipping in the back seat, she zipped open her overnight bag.

"What are you doing?"

"Changing my clothes," she said, pulling out her jeans and designer blouse, along with her fancy sneakers. "Keep your eyes up front."

He laughed, glancing in the rearview mirror as he pushed the shifter into reverse. "I saw you naked last night."

"I'm serious." She reached around her back, pulling down her zipper. Holding up her shirt, she slipped her arms out of her dress. As soon as he focused on the road in front of them, she shimmied out of her dress, pulling her top over her head and hiking up her jeans. She found her makeup case and climbed over the seat as he pulled out onto the highway. "Did I tell you we've got your father's jet?"

"You neglected to tell me that little piece of information," he said, handing her his phone. "Would you mind canceling my flight?"

"Why bother? You're going to lose your money anyway."

"Not on this airline."

She snapped her head in his direction. "Since when do you fly a discounted airline?"

"Since I don't live off my father's money."

She laughed. "Because you can afford an Absolute luxury yacht on your salary. Not to mention I saw a Harley Davidson Ultra Limited in the parking lot and Porsche, which were both your dream vehicles."

He shook his head. "All right. I've used some of my trust, but I don't live off it. I pay my own bills."

"I'm just teasing you. I might have roughed it for a few years, but that didn't stop Mommy and Daddy from sending me care packages with goodies, including a fancy coffee machine that I couldn't use and donated to the local hospital."

"You've always been a bit of a do-gooder."

"I still am, but I will admit to being spoiled, and I do enjoy flying first class."

"When you're used to being transported in the cargo hold of a C-130, a no-frills airline is first class."

"I wasn't surprised at all when I heard you'd become a fireman. You always said you wanted to become an arson investigator."

"I also said I wanted to join the military after I got my degree."

"But you dropped out of school." She flipped down the visor, exposing a small mirror so she could put on a little makeup.

"I got my degree. Six years ago, but I finished it."

"I'm glad to hear it." Puckering her lips, she applied the lip gloss, trying to ignore the pull he had over her mind and other parts.

"I've been meaning to ask. Why the Peace Corps? You never talked about that in college."

She leaned back in her seat. She could be honest, or she could lie. Her mother would tell her to fudge a little, especially if she cared about the man and wanted him in her life. Her father would tell her to be brutally honest. If he couldn't take it, he wasn't the man for her. What was odd, however, was that it had been her father who had an affair for years, so his advice didn't float.

Well, it did, just not coming from him.

"I'd planned on going back in high school, but then you and I happened, and I figured you'd be joining the Air Force after college, and having both of us living in faraway places wouldn't make for a solid foundation for a life together."

"What?" He snapped his head in her direction as he exited the highway toward the airport. "You would have given that up just because of my plans?"

"Not your plans. Our plans."

"But you never told me about this dream."

"I wanted you more than I wanted the Peace Corps," she admitted.

"But not enough to come after me when I left."

Talk about brutal, though it wasn't the truth. "We could go back and forth all day on who didn't chase after whom. I thought you'd come back to school, and when I walked into the apartment we rented for our senior year, I assumed you'd be there. But you never showed up, and that said a lot."

"I suppose it does, but maybe my leaving just opened the door for you to return to what you really wanted."

"Are you trying to pick a fight with me?" All morning he'd waffled between being nice but stand-offish or acting like he'd been annoyed by everything about her being on his boat.

The car rolled to a stop at the rental return.

"No. I'm just trying to understand because so many of your actions contradict each other." He stepped from the vehicle, giving the attendant the keys before grabbing his suitcase from the back seat.

So did his, but she wasn't about to continue this ridiculous conversation any further. They walked into the airport in a chilly silence that made her skin prickle. She glanced his way a few times, but he looked straight ahead. He did that when he was either pondering something or annoyed.

She figured right now he was both.

"We go through the main security, then we get a bus over to the small airplane hangar. The crew is on the jet and ready to go."

"I haven't flown on a plush private jet since my dad took the golf team to the Bahamas."

"Do you still get to play?" she asked, stepping

into the airport security line through pre-check, grateful the conversation shifted quickly and easily.

"I play when I can. How about you?" He dumped his bag on the conveyor belt and stepped through the metal detector. He didn't look back as she followed suit.

She gathered her things and headed toward the bus terminal. "Not since the last time with you."

"Well, maybe we should play a round at the club while I'm home. I've always enjoyed the way you cock your hip right before you swing."

She stepped through the door he held open and climbed onto the bus. Her stomach pitched and rolled. And here he thought her actions were conflicting. He sent her one mixed message after the other, and it felt more like watching a tennis match than having a conversation.

"That right there is why I don't play."

"It's even better when you bend over to pick up your ball."

"All right. That's enough." She let out a long sigh. "You go from being pissy about what I did or didn't do years ago to flirting with me. We had our fun last night to bring us closure. Either close it, or… or… just fucking close it, okay?"

"Why don't you tell me how you really feel?" he

said, holding the bar in the center of the bus over his seat next to her. "Oh, wait. You don't know how you really feel."

"Well, neither do you."

The rest of the ride was spent in silence, as was boarding his father's jet. She'd chosen to fly with a skeleton crew, just the pilot and copilot. This made Rex insanely happy as he poured himself a scotch on the rocks before takeoff. In all the years she'd known him, she'd never seen him drink before noon, at the earliest, and that was only when they had a football party or major family gathering.

She opted for coffee.

He leaned back in the seat across from her, swirling his drink, the ice cubes clinking against the glass. The plane leveled out, and the captain came over the loudspeaker, letting them know the estimated arrival time and the current weather in Maryland.

"I'm sorry," Rex said, still staring at his drink. "I'm nervous about being around family, and I'm taking it out on you."

"Thank you, but it's more than that. You've been upset with me ever since I stepped from your bedroom this morning." She fluffed her hair as if that would give her a shot of confidence. "I don't regret what happened, but I'd understand if you did."

"That's not it at all." He set the glass down and looked directly at her. "I'm glad we had last night. We couldn't get past our stubbornness back then, but we each did things to remind ourselves of what we didn't fight for, and I find myself wondering why and wanting more. Only, your life is in Maryland, and mine's in Florida, and neither one of us is going to change that."

"What do you mean?" She clutched the leaf pendant dangling from her neck, fingering the silver piece of jewelry. She wasn't so sure she wanted the answer, but she needed it.

"We held on to each other in different ways, but we went about the lives we both wanted to live. We didn't really think twice about it. We felt guilty about choosing our goals, so we tortured ourselves with constant reminders. You did it with tattoos and I did with possessions. We must choose one, and we both know what that will be, even if we wanted a redo."

She stared at him for a long moment, digesting his words. She wanted to argue that they were immature and young. That they didn't have the skill set to deal with what happened in their lives, but deep down, she knew he had a valid point. Only, he failed to comprehend that she would have never become a Peace Corps Volunteer had he not left her. Sure, she would have found some way to do service work, though it would have been local. Or wherever he was stationed. And there could have been opportunities in the military for her passion to help others.

But what would be the point in telling him that he didn't want her in his life when it was painfully obvious? His whole concept of a potential redo was ridiculous. That rambling didn't make sense. Sure, the sex was great. They still fit together like an old pair of gloves. But it wasn't something they could slide back into.

Too much time and too much hurt.

"I get it and agree." She nodded.

"I'm sorry if this is hurting you," he said.

Now she just wanted to throttle him. "I'm not hurt. Why would you even think that?"

"I don't know." He raised his free hand, letting it fall into his lap. "I'm telling you that what happened last night won't happen again because our lives are too different, even though I do still care for you."

"Wow. That was really hard for you to say, wasn't it?" She twisted her hair between her fingers.

"It's coming out all wrong," he said.

"You can say that again," she mumbled. "Look. I don't want anything from you. And for the record, I will always care about you. That's obvious. But both of us are different people with our own lives. I believe this was good for us. Call it closure. Call it moving forward. I don't care. But I'm not looking for anything other than maybe not being angry with each other anymore."

He reached out and squeezed her hand. "I think I can manage that."

"Good."

"Are we getting a car service, or is someone picking us up?"

"Your father and his wife."

"I've never met her," he said, dropping his head back. "The few times I've seen my dad, I've always asked if it could just be us. I know that's selfish, but it felt weird to accept her, when I'm an unaccepting asshole about everything else."

Tilly laughed. "She's a nice lady and makes your father happy."

"How does she feel about my dad taking care of

his ex-wife?" Every word was laced with a bit of kick as if they'd been drenched in Tabasco sauce.

"She's actually taking care of the day-to-day things, spending her days with your mom, cooking and cleaning."

"That's just weird."

"So is the fact that you had sex last night with your stepsister." She smiled, cocking her head.

"I can't believe you said that. Out loud."

"It's a fact. My dad did marry your mom," she said. "And even though their affair hurt a lot of people, in the end, they were very much in love."

"I don't know what you expect me to do with that statement."

"It wasn't easy for me either." She held his gaze. "There were lots of tears, lots of yelling, doors slamming, and fighting. You name it, we all did it. But at the end of the day, we chose to be a family, and we all have missed you."

5

R ex followed Tilly across the tarmac toward a stretch limo, trying to diffuse the pain that tore through his heart. He couldn't tell if Tilly had put it there or his family.

Or both.

His heart had taken a mini beating the moment he opened his eyes this morning to see her sprawled out on top of him in his bed. Her long hair flowed across his chest, and her arms and legs were tangled up with his. Visions of leisurely walks along the beach, children frolicking in the ocean waves, maybe even a dog chasing a Frisbee teased his mind.

Those were all dreams of the past and now he was walking right into where it had all begun.

The limo's back door opened, and his father stepped out into the humid air. His hair had thinned and grayed, but his muscular frame filled out his dress slacks and shirt exactly as Rex had remembered. His father held out his hand as a woman stepped from the vehicle. She wore a stunning light-blue pantsuit. Her short brown hair was perfectly styled. From a distance, he couldn't even fathom a guess at her age, but she was in her early sixties from the few talks he'd had with his father and siblings.

"Judy is her name, right?" he whispered. His palms grew clammy, and his pulse jackhammered in his chest.

"That's correct," Tilly said, slowing her pace. She rested her hand in the crook of his elbow. Instinctively, he raised his forearm. "She was married to a banker for twenty years."

"Do I have more stepsiblings I need to be aware of?"

Tilly let out a soft laugh. "No. She never had children."

"Why'd she get divorced?"

"She didn't. She was widowed."

He swallowed. That was good information to

know. Otherwise, he might go and make an ass of himself by saying something stupid.

The last ten paces, he took deep, calming breaths.

"Dad," he said, extending his hand.

"Rex." His father pushed his hand aside and pulled him in for a tight, slightly too long hug. "You look good, boy."

"So do you, Dad."

"Tilly. Dear Tilly. Thanks for talking him into coming home." His father took Tilly into his arms, kissing her cheek.

"My pleasure," Tilly said.

"Judy. I'd like you to meet my son, Rex." His father beamed with pride just like the day Rex graduated from high school. His father had always been his biggest supporter, even when Rex said no to a prep school offer to play golf and even a chance to go professional. While Rex loved the sport, he didn't want to make it his living, no matter how good at it he was, and he was still a scratch golfer. Not bad for a guy who only played on weekends, and not every weekend because that would cut into his fishing.

"Nice to meet you, ma'am," Rex said.

She took the hand he extended but leaned in for an awkward hug. "Please don't call me ma'am or

Mrs. Jordan because that would be more awkward than this. Judy is just fine."

A nervous laugh trickled out of his mouth. "I'm sorry I was unable to make the wedding. I really was deployed at the time." There was no reason he needed to qualify that, and by the wrinkled brow on his father's head, Rex had not only insulted him by implying they didn't believe his response, but it also reminded everyone that Rex hadn't been home in ten years.

"Thank you for your service," Judy said with a poised smile.

He wanted to hate the woman as much as he resented his parents for destroying what he believed had been the perfect marriage. The perfect family.

"You're welcome." His heart ached for what he had once been and what a fool he'd been. He hadn't chased after Tilly because he wanted to follow his dream. No. He didn't stay to make it work because he was afraid and made it impossible for her to come after him.

He swallowed. Hard.

But his parents had betrayed him, a thought that still burned a hole in his gut. Even now, he could perfectly recall the day he'd found his mother with Mr. Bettencourt. A son, no matter the age, doesn't unsee something like that. He wondered if he'd found out some other way and didn't have to be the one to tell his father if he would have reacted differently.

He slipped into the limo, Tilly sitting next to him, his father and Judy sitting across. His lungs burned with every breath he took. His father and his father's wife were strangers to him. He had no idea what to say, much less how to act.

"Your father tells me you left the Air Force and now work for something called the Aegis Network." She patted his father's leg. "Gerry, did I get that right?"

His father nodded, staring at Rex with questioning eyes, though what they questioned, Rex didn't know.

"He also tells me you're in some training or school to be an arson investigator with the local fire department. That must be fascinating."

Rex arched a brow. "How'd you know about that, Dad?"

"You've forgotten I know Decker Rigg's father."

"Keeping tabs on me?"

Tilly pinched him, and he flinched, though not necessarily at the physical pain.

He deserved more of a pinch since the words

tumbled out of his mouth before he could think about how they would sound.

"Sorry, Dad. That's not what I meant." He rubbed the side of his leg and laced his fingers through Tilly's.

She tried to pull back, but he didn't let her. He needed her warmth and her strength if he was going to get through this without being too much of an ass.

"You meant it like that. I was always up your ass about everything when you were a teenager and worse when you went to college." His father smiled, shaking his head. "Remember when I tried to bribe your academic advisor to give me your grades when you refused to sign off on them?"

"You were a bit of a control freak." The corner of Rex's mouth twitched into a smile. "I purposely maintained a status quo average just to annoy you."

"I know. Smart-ass kid," his father said.

"I know an adult who is just like that," Judy said with a bright smile.

It was impossible to hate the woman. She seemed perfect for his dad, and he really had no reason to dislike her. She hadn't done anything wrong. She hadn't broken up a marriage.

Fuck. He needed to change his attitude and his thinking.

A long, thick silence filled the limo. Rex looked out the window as they pulled into a familiar neighborhood. Not his old one, or Tilly's, since his mom and her dad had bought a new place together, but it was only a couple of neighborhoods away and still within the country club. That had to be awkward at the Holiday Ball.

"Thanks for coming," his father said with a throaty tone, his eyes glossed over, threatening to tear. "I won't pretend to understand how you felt ten years ago. I had my pain to grapple with, and I don't think I was a very good father to you or your siblings during the divorce. But I know what this will mean to your mother."

"She doesn't know I'm coming?"

Tilly squeezed his hand. "She's been asking for you, and we all said we'd try to find you, but we didn't want to get her hopes up."

"I hope I don't give her a heart attack," Rex mumbled.

"That's not funny," his father said, though there was a lightness to the words.

"It's inappropriately funny." Rex coughed, nearly choking on the phrase his mother used to toss out whenever the locker room talk got out of hand or a sexist joke would be told in front of her.

The limo pulled into a house on the fifth tee box. "They bought old man Walker's place?"

"You didn't know that?" Tilly questioned.

"There are many things I don't know," he admitted, his insides fluttering like a dog's tail. "I know this is no excuse, but my life in the Air Force was filled with more deployments than being Stateside. Even after I left the military, this organization I joined, the Aegis Network, has me traveling a lot. And then there is my work as a firefighter. I don't have much downtime."

"So we've been told." His father's voice boomed with pride once again.

Rex snapped his head, catching his father's gaze. Rex expected a lecture on how easy it was in today's age to maintain contact, not genuine delight from a man who seemed to relish in his son's accomplishments, even if from a distance.

"Why don't I go see how Louisa is doing?" Judy pushed open the limo door. "Should I prepare her for Rex's visit?"

"No," his father said, maintaining eye contact with Rex. "I'd like it if you told her you came to see her on your own. You can tell her I sent Tilly to talk you into it if you want, since we've had that conversation. But remember, when someone knows the end is near, they look back over their lives and all the regrets and pain that come with it, and it haunts their existence." He leaned over, putting a strong hand on Rex's knee. "What she did was wrong, and it hurt us all. This is no excuse, but our marriage had been over for years. We stayed together for you kids. Maybe that was a big mistake."

Rex couldn't stand to listen to reason for a second longer. "I'm here. Let's just leave it at that." As he stepped from the limo, the warm sun hit his face. Golf carts rolled across the cart path. The sound of an iron hitting a ball played like music in his ears. He ducked his head back into the limo. "What are the chances I could get a round of golf in after I visit with Mom?"

"I'll set it up," his father said.

"Thanks." He turned and faced old man Walker's house, which was now his mother's house. "Well, here goes nothing."

He stuffed his hands in his pockets and stood at the front door. Did he knock? Ring the doorbell? Walk in? Thankfully, he didn't have to make that decision as Judy appeared and opened the front door.

"She's awake and knows something is up, but I doubt she knows you're here." Judy placed her hand on his shoulder. "She's been hopeful that you would come home, but she also understands why you wouldn't. She doesn't blame you. Only herself."

That damn near broke his heart. "Can I ask you a question?" He actually had a million of them, but he wasn't sure half mattered anymore.

"What is it?" Judy stepped back, waving a hand into a sitting room to the right of the foyer. He recognized the white sofa from Tilly's parents' house, but only because they'd had sex on it once.

Or twice.

Pictures of both families lined the floor-to-ceiling bookcases. It was strange to see his family portrait, with both his parents in it, displayed next to one of Tilly's with all of her siblings and parents.

"If you've more than one, why don't we sit."

He shook his head, reaching for the frame with a dozen small pictures of him and Tilly growing up as kids.

"Your mother has a collection of picture frames like that one throughout the house. She's still holding out for a reunion with the two of you."

Maybe he should tell his mother that his love for Tilly would be forever tainted because of her actions, and they'd get back together when hell froze over.

God, he was a mess. One minute he wanted nothing more than to be with Tilly. The next he just wanted to continue to hurt everyone.

Mostly himself.

Living a tormented life had become the only way he knew how to survive.

Being in this house, surrounded by images of family and love, made him want to run and scream naked through the neighborhood like a crazy person. But the worst part was that he was a grown man, not a child, and he had no right to begrudge his parents' happiness or to judge their decisions.

And none of it had to do with giving his mother some peace before she passed.

"I hope you don't mind if I'm blunt," he said.

"I'm your mother's primary caregiver, I'm used to blunt."

He let out a short laugh. "How do you do it? I mean, taking care of your husband's ex-wife. That's got to be hard."

"It might have been if I knew them during the divorce, but I didn't. I only saw two people who stopped loving each other but never stopped loving their kids." Judy ran her fingers across an old Victorian desk. "Your parents have become friends. Close friends. I'd be a bitch if I stood between two people who have shared so much joy and heartache." She closed the gap, reaching out and curling her fingers around his biceps. "They became close over their shared grief of hurting and losing you. Your father believes he was just as much at fault for that as your mother. They both love you very much, but they are about as stubborn as a baby that is unwilling to walk."

"That's a family trait."

"Anything else?"

"Just point me in the direction of my mother," he said. If he didn't do this now, he'd never do it.

"Upstairs and down the hallway. You'll walk right into the master bedroom. I should warn you, she's weak and doesn't look well. She's lost a ton of weight and is quite pale."

"That has to drive her insane. She always loved a good tan."

"She demands tanning lotion every day."

"That sounds like my mother." He left Judy standing in the sitting room as he climbed the staircase. The hallway walls were filled with more photos and familiar furniture from both his childhood home and Tilly's.

I slept with my stepsister.

Well, she was his girlfriend before that, and it didn't matter anyway.

He raised his trembling hand and knocked on the door.

"Come in," his mother's voice rang out as soft and sweet as he remembered. At nine years old, he broke his wrist snow skiing on a family vacation. It had been displaced and had to be reset. His mother talked to him through the entire process, telling him stories of her childhood and the crazy things his grandfather used to do. By the time the doctor was done, he'd barely known he'd been hurt, thanks to his loving mother.

He sucked in a deep breath and told himself this would be easier than running into a burning building.

Right.

He stepped through door, mentally preparing himself. "Hey, Ma," he said as she came into view. She was propped up in her bed, a food tray over her legs. Her once long, thick hair had thinned and turned gray. She wasn't as pale as he thought she'd be, but her frail body sucker punched his ability to take another step.

All the anger and resentment melted from his body.

She turned her head, raising a small sandwich. Her hand fell to the tray, sending the plate with the rest of the food onto the bed.

He raced to her side, quickly cleaning up the mess, thankful no liquid had been spilled. He set her food off to the side and sat on the edge of the bed. "Surprise?" He didn't think his heart could ache more, but seeing his strong, sophisticated mother in such a vulnerable state drove home how much he'd missed out on during the last ten years.

She blinked a few times, shaking her head. "Now I'm delusional," she whispered.

"No. I'm really here." He took his mother's feeble hand in his, rubbing gently.

"I can't decide whether to hug or slap you."

"How about both?"

She raised her arm and patted the side of his cheek. "If you weren't so damned pretty, I'd really smack you."

He leaned in, drawing his mother close, being careful not to hurt her, but she had other things in mind as she nearly crushed him with a hug and slobbered on his cheek with a million pecks like she used to do when he was a small boy and he'd run away trying to brush them off, totally embarrassed she'd done that in front of his friends.

"You need to shave." His mother leaned back, folding her arms over her chest.

"I didn't have much time this morning. We just landed less than an hour ago."

"Tilly got you to come home." Her mother waggled a finger under his nose. "And don't lie to me. I'm not that fragile, and I'm not dead yet."

He swallowed the sob that smacked the back of his throat and willed the tears glossing over his eyes to fade away. "She had something to do with it."

"Your father sent her. He doesn't think I know, even though I might have suggested she was the only one who could do it. He has it in his head that I needed you to come home on your own. But screw that. I'll take it any way I can. Besides, you and Tilly belong together. Oh, the babies you two will make. They will be spectacular."

He shook his head. "I didn't think you could get any more candid, but you have, and you've developed a very dry sense of humor."

"Losing your son, then your second husband, and now dying, will do that to a woman."

"You didn't lose me," he mumbled, wondering

if she was trying to hurt him, or just being inappropriately honest.

"Yeah. Actually, I did. After I got the last letter you sent me a year after you'd left, I realized how badly I handled the situation and that you would never forgive me. And don't go saying that you do just because you think it's what a dying woman wants to hear because it's not. I just wanted to see you and have the chance to tell you I'm sorry. In person."

"Apology accepted." He leaned in and kissed her cheek. Even in death, she still smelled like roses. "I'm sure I owe you a few."

"You owe Tilly a lot more than me." His mother tilted her head slightly to the left, pursed her lips, and gave him that look that dared him to argue with her.

"We talked."

"And?"

"There is no and. Tilly and I were over long ago. We've both moved on."

"Really? Do you have a girlfriend?"

He opened his mouth, but she didn't let him speak.

"I bet you don't, and if you lie to me, I'll know it."

"I've had girlfriends."

"But they don't last, do they? And Tilly has horrible taste in men. God-awful."

He laughed. "I can't speak for her, but I'm happy with my life and I don't need a girlfriend for that."

"Because anyone you date isn't right for you. Tilly has always been the one, and I'm going to get the two of you back together if it's the last thing I do. I owe you and her that. What I really want in my last days is to see the two of you together again. My actions destroyed that and now I'm going to fix it."

The last thing he wanted to do was hurt his mother. But he couldn't lie. Not now. Not ever. "I'm sorry, Ma, but it's not going to happen. Tilly and I got the chance to talk about the way in which we hurt each other. But we're different people now. There's nothing there anymore."

"Talk is cheap. How long are you here for?"

"Couple of days. But I'll come back as often as I can." Words he hadn't expected to come out of his mouth, but he wouldn't take them back. He desperately wanted to be there for his mother. For himself. He wanted to be at her bedside and he would do whatever he could to make that happen.

"I need you to do me a favor."

"Whatever you need," he said, thankful they were off the Tilly topic.

"While you're here, take Tilly out on a couple of dates. See how——"

"Mom. Do you really want to start a fight on my first day back in over ten years? Because I don't. I'm here because I want to be. Not because Tilly asked me to, but because I realized I needed to make things right with you. I'm truly sorry. I shouldn't have stayed away so long."

She straightened her spine, sitting up taller. "What harm could it do to take her out and show her a good time?"

Little did his mother know that his heart was already bleeding out.

"And it will make a dying woman happy."

"Fine," he said a little too quickly, but it put a smile on his mother's face, and he preferred that to a scowl.

"Good. Now, why don't you go play some golf with your father? Then we can all have dinner together tonight. Afterward, you can take Tilly out for drinks, a movie, or maybe a romantic stroll."

He kissed his mother's cheek, helping her fluff her pillow as she shifted lower in the bed. He snagged the food tray and headed for the stairs with a funny tickle across his skin. It wasn't an unpleasant feeling, but it certainly was an unwelcoming one.

When he got to the bottom of the stairs and rounded the corner, he was greeted by Tilly and his father.

"How'd things go?" his father asked.

"It was interesting. She forgives me and I can honestly say I've put the past behind me. I plan on coming home as often as possible until the bitter end. But she certainly knows how to play the dying card."

"What the hell does that mean?" Tilly asked, snapping her hip to the side in an indignant gesture.

"She knew Dad sent you to get me, and her dying wish wasn't for my forgiveness but for the two of us to get back together. While I'm here, I've been ordered to date you."

His father bent over, slapped his leg, and burst out laughing.

"I don't see what is so funny," Rex said, scowling.

"Your mother always gets her way." His father glanced between Rex and Tilly. "And she's always right."

"Not this time," Tilly said. "I can't believe I fell for her tricks!" She folded her arms. "I'm sorry, Gerry. I flew all the way to Florida because you asked me to since she so desperately wanted to make peace with her son. But no, the reality is she's still trying to play matchmaker. How many times have I told her that ship has sailed? That he and I are over. We have absolutely no feelings left for one another. None. Zilch. This is crazy. She can't make me date him. I'm not letting her play the death card. Again."

His father stopped laughing.

Judy stared at Tilly with a perplexed expression.

Rex cleared his throat. "Okay. What am I missing? Why are you so pissed off?"

"I don't like being manipulated."

"You knew this was what she wanted?"

"She might have mentioned it a time or two." Tilly cocked her head. "And come on, do you seriously want to date me while you're here spending time with your mom?"

"Going out and seeing the old stomping grounds wouldn't be the worst idea." He shrugged.

"You are one big pain in my ass." She turned and stomped out the front door.

Rex's dad squeezed his shoulder. "Your mom

has been putting some pressure on her about you. Pulling out old photo albums. Reminiscing about prom. Chatting about the time we caught you kids on the third fairway having—"

"Don't say it, Dad." Rex stuck his finger in his ear and wiggled it. "That's not really fair of Mom to do to Tilly. It wasn't easy for her to come to collect me, and I made it even harder."

"I'm sure you did," his dad said. "If I had known what your mother intended, I would have come myself." He lowered his chin. "But let's call the kettle black here, son. Would you have come if anyone other than Tilly had shown up?"

"I don't know," Rex answered honestly. "That woman is not only persuasive, but she's also a stubborn mule who wouldn't get off my boat until she either drowned in a storm or I agreed. I couldn't let her ruin her expensive dress, so I relented." He rubbed the back of his neck and let out a long breath. "For Mom's sake, she'll go out with me. But sadly, it's going to be all for show."

"If you say so, son."

6

"Your golf game has gotten better." Rex took the glass of scotch his father offered and settled into one of the outdoor chairs in front of one of three fire pits. The evening sun lowered toward the horizon.

"I kind of wish yours had gotten worse. You'd think with how little you played, it would catch up to you."

"I gave you nine strokes." Rex laughed.

"And I still lost."

"I once went an entire year without seeing a golf course and was invited to play with my CO. I shot a 70 on a course that was a par 71. My CO was quite happy I was his partner and lived up to my reputation."

His father shifted his gaze. "I know it took you a lot to come home." He stared into his glass while swirling the dark liquid. "I appreciate it as much as your mother does."

"If I'm being honest, I'm glad I'm here. It's uncomfortable and my emotions are all over the place, but I would have regretted not coming."

"I'm glad to hear that."

He stared at his father, studying every line on his face. He noticed how he sipped his drink and Rex realized he did it precisely the same way. "I have to be honest here, son. I can't help but wonder if you would have ever made it back without the nudge from Tilly, which makes me wonder if your mother isn't right about the two of you."

"I bought a plane ticket. More than once. I would have gotten the courage to come without you sending Tilly."

"You say that, but yet you didn't get on the plane. It took Tilly showing up and dragging your ass home." His father lifted his hand. "Since your mom got sick, Judy and I have been the ones to take care of her—well, mostly Judy. When it came down to it, I wanted to be the one to come slap some sense into you. It would have been easy for me to leave for a few days thanks to the patience of my lovely bride. But if we're being brutally honest, I knew that Tilly would be the one who got through to you."

Rex laughed. "I certainly was shocked to see her, although I knew exactly what her purpose was, and I had my arsenal of reasons why I wouldn't go ready."

"What changed your mind?"

"I'm tired of running from the past. Of being angry at all of you. Don't get me wrong, I still struggle with it. I have a million resentments. I'm not over some of them. But for the sake of Mom, I can move past them and begin to mend fences."

"Of all my kids, you've always been the most sensitive and the first to put up walls. When all this happened, I told your mother to give you space, and she warned me that if we gave you too much, you'd be lost to us forever."

"Yeah, but if you had pushed me too hard, I would have gone farther away than joining the Air Force." He raised his glass and took a hearty sip. "There was no winning with me in this situation. I found Mom and Tilly's dad together. It's a vision I will never get out of my head. But what made it worse was Mom trying to explain it away. As if my eyes had deceived me. And then she begged me not to tell you."

"It was a terrible position for her to put you in. No doubt. I wish you hadn't found out, but you have to understand, I already knew."

"That doesn't make me feel any better, Dad." Rex shifted in his seat. "And when you told me that after you moved out of the house, it only served to piss me off even more."

"What I'm about to share might ruin what little relationship we have left, but I feel at this point, there are things that might help you understand mine and your mother's dynamic at the time a little better."

"I'm really not sure I want to hear this."

"Look. The one thing your mom always gave me kudos for was being a good dad. But she thought I was a shit husband. And that's a true statement. I was so wrapped up in making my millions that I neglected her and our marriage. I would go on business trips, leaving her home to deal with the children. When I would come home, my focus was on playing golf and hanging with you kids. We didn't do date nights. She was lonely."

"That's no excuse to have an affair."

"You're right, it's not. But she wasn't the only one." His father arched a brow.

"Excuse me?" Rex aggressively set his glass down on the counter. "You stepped out on Mom? With whom?" He waved his hand. "Never mind. I don't want to know."

"It wasn't with anyone you kids would have known. And sadly, there was more than one woman. I'm not proud. Actually, I'm mortified and ashamed of my actions. I came from nothing and here I was, a self-made man, playing with the big boys. I'd go on these trips, and women—well, they'd be available."

"Jesus, Dad. You're right. I don't want to hear this." Rex ran a hand over his face. "Did Mom know?"

"Not at first. But something in me switched. Guilt ate me alive. I had the perfect life and I was pissing it away. I thought if I changed, I could make things right. I started traveling less. Playing less golf. But it was too late. The damage in my marriage was already done. All your mother and I did was argue. We'd fight over money. Over you kids. Hell, we fought over how I parked my damn sports car in the garage. Honestly, I blamed myself for her affair."

Rex lifted his drink and took a big gulp. "Not

your fault, but damn, you and Mom knew how to put on a good show. Everyone thought you two had the perfect everything."

"That's money talking," his dad said. "We decided to wait to separate until all of you were out of college. We thought it would be less traumatizing. But it was getting harder and harder to play the game. The reality is, we should have divorced when you were in middle school. That's on us, not you."

Rex wasn't sure what to do with all this information. He allowed his mind to pull up memories from his childhood and if he was being honest, he could see his parents' misery. The coldness that lived in his house. It was never directed at him. Both his folks showered him with love. Genuine, honest love.

But they didn't do that with each other.

"Can I ask you something?" Rex said.

"Of course."

"Are you happy now?"

"Not completely, no. You cutting us all off has taken a toll on that." His father held up a hand. "I don't blame you for that, and I can't imagine what it must have been like for you, but the pain of knowing your son is a phone call away, and he won't answer, well, that has hurt. A lot."

"But you lived your life. Got remarried."

"And look at you," his father said with a wave of his hand. "You've become a mighty fine man, but are you happy?"

He sipped his drink, letting the burn of the alcohol glide across his throat. "I'm not unhappy."

His father let out a short laugh. "That's a nonanswer."

"It's the same one you gave."

"Not exactly," his father said. "I love my wife. We have a good life together. We enjoy golfing. Boating. Fishing. She's been so good to your mom. Your siblings. My grandkids. But every day I wake up and think about the son who was hurt in the worst way and it kills me that no matter what I've tried to make it right, you've stayed away. If I had told you about the kind of man I was when you were little, would that have changed things?"

"It might have made things worse. I might have resented you as much as I resented her," Rex admitted. "I'd honestly like to leave the past in the rearview. I'm here now. I can't promise you that I won't get angry or that things won't bubble to the surface, but I'm committed to making things right. I don't want to live this way anymore. I've come to understand that it's not worth holding on to this grudge any longer."

His father reached out and squeezed his forearm. "I know you think your mother's nuts for wanting you and Tilly to date for the time you are here. She feels responsible for your breakup. Always has. And you know, Tilly's father felt the same way."

Rex breathed slowly. "That's one of the things that will keep coming to the surface. I can't help it. Whenever I look back, I'm still angry. Not because of you or Mom, but because Tilly didn't seem to care what my mother and her father were doing to our families."

"Of course she cared, but because she stuck around, she saw how jovial her father had become, and over time, we all developed an odd friendship. But it didn't happen overnight. If you had been here, you would have seen how everyone struggled. I always say how I wish we had ended our marriage when you kids were young, but I can't change the past. And there are good things that came out of it."

"I have no idea how you can say that." Rex raised his glass in a sarcastic cheers.

"That's where you refuse to see the bigger picture. Had we divorced back then, you and Tilly might have never happened, and she was the best damn thing that ever happened to you. I agree with your mother. You need to give you and Tilly a second chance."

"Jesus, I can't believe you just said that. It's one thing to take her out to put a smile on Mom's face, but you really expect me to do anything but pretend?"

"True love—the kind that never dies—doesn't happen all the time," his father said. "I care deeply for your mother. She gave me three beautiful children and our life together had some good times. But we didn't have that kind of love. She found it with Tilly's father and I found it with Judy."

Rex groaned.

"I know that's a tough pill to swallow. But let's get serious. Your mom and I were pressured to get married. She was pregnant and I was told that's what I was supposed to do. I don't regret it. Any of it. I can't because I wouldn't have you or your brother or sister. You and Tilly might have been young, but I know real love when I see it and it's still there if you let it fill that closed off heart of yours."

Rex set his glass on the table and stood. "No offense, Dad, but you don't know me. I'm not the same man who walked away."

"Maybe not. But I know Tilly."

Rex shook his head. "Perhaps, but I don't really know any of you anymore, so I'd appreciate it if you'd back off the Tilly thing. I'll take Tilly out for Mom, but I won't pretend I still have feelings for her."

Actually, he'd have to pretend not to have any feelings for her, at least to himself.

Tilly smoothed down the front of her miniskirt, doing a one-hundred-eighty-degree turn in front of the mirror. Louisa had been kind enough to let her keep some of her things in the bedroom she'd called home between college and her travels with the Peace Corps before getting her own apartment in Bethesda. Since Louisa had gotten sick, Tilly had made a point of coming home every weekend and tried to make it home for dinner at least once a week.

Gathering her hair and holding it behind her head, she contemplated putting it up.

Rex preferred it down.

She reached for a ponytail holder and a clip. Twisting her hair, she pulled it back, leaving a few strands out to fan her face. Satisfied that Rex would hate her outfit and her hair, she left the comfort of her bedroom and made her way downstairs. Dinner would certainly prove to be interesting to say the very least. She knew Louisa would play match-maker, but what she didn't count on was Rex's willingness to play along.

Keyword: Play.

"Don't you look stunning," Louisa said, sitting at the head of the table in the dining room, her IV drip perched next to her. Louisa did her best to look as pretty as possible by wearing a little makeup, styling what hair she had left, and wearing designer shawls to cover her comfortable pajamas that didn't give her bed sores. Most nights she actually ate in her room with Judy, a staff nurse, or one of her friends who came to visit. But when the family showed up, she did her best to make it to the dinner table.

"She's always the prettiest girl in the room," Judy said, sitting to the left of Louisa, Gerry in the seat to the right.

The table sat ten comfortably, and her father had always sat at the opposite end, but no one ever sat there now and the waitstaff never set a place setting.

God, she missed her dad. He'd been her rock, even when she hated him for what he'd done. There'd been so many tears. So many fights. So many threats of never speaking to him again. But when she saw how happy her dad and Louisa were together, she couldn't bring herself to cut them off like Rex had.

She wanted her family. Needed them. Numerous therapy sessions later, she'd learned to forgive.

Tilly wasn't quite sure where to sit. Most dinners included other family members that scattered around the table, giving her plenty of options. She usually sat next to Judy, but what if Rex wanted to be across from his father?

"This is all wrong," Louisa said, waving her arms frantically. "Judy, dear. You should be sitting next to your adoring husband so the two lovebirds can play footsie under the table."

Swallowing the sarcastic remark, Tilly took her seat, leaving a space between her and Rex's mother, while Judy scurried across the room to be by Gerry. If someone had told Tilly twelve years ago that she'd be forced to date Rex, she would have laughed hysterically at the absurdity of it. She'd loved him back then, so she thought they'd be together forever.

Now she just wanted to get this over with, even though her heart was still filled with the same love that had never died.

She figured maybe three or four dates and they'd be able to say they'd given it the good old college try but that the spark no longer lingered.

Shit, she didn't want to do that to Louisa. She knew what this meant to Rex's mom. The dating would have to last as long as she did.

"Where is the prodigal son?" Tilly asked.

Louisa gasped.

"I didn't mean it that way." But she really had. Her frustration level was at the breaking point. One more *cutest couple* comment, and she'd blow up like the Fourth of July.

"Are you sure about that?" Rex's voice startled her, making her jump.

She looked over her shoulder. He leaned against the doorjamb sporting a pink button-down shirt, black slacks, and a pair of dark boat shoes. He'd always been the best dressed person in any room. Not to mention the hottest. Girls drooled over him, constantly trying to get him to notice them, but during all the years they dated, he never once turned his head.

He was a good boyfriend that way.

Actually, in every way.

"There he is." His mother patted the chair next to her. "Judy poured a nice bottle of red. I can't have any, but if I recall correctly, you had your father's taste for wine."

"I still do." Rex sauntered across the room, eyeing her with a devilish twinkle in his eye like the night he'd taken her to a fancy restaurant and then made love to her on the beach, listening the waves crash against the sand.

She hated that look. It always meant he was up to no good.

"I also still hate your hair like this." He snagged the clip holding her hair up before tugging at her ponytail.

"Ouch." She balked, but he'd always been good at taking her hair out of an updo without pulling the strands out. "I can't believe you just did that. It took an hour for me to get the right look, and how dare you be so bullish as to take it down."

He tossed her accessories on the hutch on the other side of the room. "You knew I would, which is why you wore your hair that way."

Louisa scowled. "Children. Stop your bickering."

"I wore it that way because I don't like eating my hair," she said, trying to diffuse the situation. The last thing she wanted to do was upset his mother, though that was his doing, not hers.

He looped his arm over her chair, leaning in, his hot breath warming her skin. "You just wanted my fingers in it again," he whispered, but not soft enough because his mother's frown turned to a smile wider than the state of Texas.

He took his seat, keeping that stupid grin on his face.

When Louisa left the table, Tilly was going to lay into Rex. It was one thing to date for the benefit of his mother, but it was entirely another thing to turn it into a display at the dinner table.

"Stop it," she said behind gritted teeth, kicking him under the table.

He took that as it was okay to pat her thigh.

She glared at him with a smile. "What's for dinner tonight?" she asked, turning her attention to his mother.

"I had the cook make Rex's favorite." Louisa rang the bell on the table. A little old-fashioned, but the staff didn't seem to mind. Besides, Louisa treated everyone with kindness and respect. She not only paid well and gave everyone generous bonuses and lots of time off, but she made them part of the family.

"Oh, I love blackened salmon," his father said, raising his glass. "I'd like to make a toast."

This should be rich.

She held her wine up, waiting to down it in one gulp.

"To family." He lifted his arm higher.

"That's it?" Louisa asked.

"I think that says it all," Gerry said.

"I'll drink to that." She didn't bother to clink with anyone. The tart red liquid burned as it flowed from her throat to her stomach. She wasn't even sure if she actually swallowed, much less tasted anything. "I'm ready for another."

Everyone at the table stared at her with a perfectly arched brow.

Thankfully, Rex filled her glass, though not as high as she would have liked, but really, she needed to slow down and get a grip. It was all just fake dating. She and Rex were over. They had one night to say their official goodbye. It wasn't anything other than great sex. He'd made that perfectly clear.

The courses came and went, and the conversation seemed to stay off whether or not she and Rex were made for each other. She enjoyed listening to Rex's tales from his service in the military, his new job, and the fires he fought, though he did say, *I can't talk about that,* a lot.

By the time the after-dinner coffee was served, but before dessert, it was obvious to everyone that Louisa was exhausted, even though she kept trying to say she was fine.

"Let's get you up to bed," Gerry said. He was so good with his Louisa and it warmed Tilly's heart how this family could come together in the end for Louisa.

Tilly had her fair share of resentment toward Louisa in the early days. They had their own disagreements, but Louisa had been kind and patient. Loving even.

"You should be saying that to your current wife, not your ex-wife," Louisa said, teasing.

He smiled. "As soon as we get you upstairs, I plan on taking her home and—"

"Dad," Rex said with a scrunched nose. "This is just too weird for me."

Gerry laughed. "Welcome back to the nuthouse, son."

"I'll help." Judy rose, guiding Louisa out of the chair.

"Good night, son." Louisa hugged Rex.

A warmth spread over Tilly's heart seeing Rex embrace his mother again. She really needed to relax and just get with his mother's program for the week. After that, Rex would be gone. Sure, he'd be back and the dance would start all over again, but she'd have a reprieve. Time and space to go back to her life and forget about Rex, until the pretending had to commence again.

"I've had the staff make the bed in the room next to Tilly's. I think you'll be comfortable there."

Tilly coughed, burning her lips on the hot coffee she'd just brought to her lips. "That's a shared bathroom."

"I know. I didn't want the cleaning people to have to deal with another one. This is just easier." Louisa patted her shoulder. "Stop fighting it, dear. Trust me. By the end of the week, you're going to realize how madly in love you two still are."

She opened her mouth, but snapped it shut. Nothing good would come from saying exactly what she was thinking. Leaning across the table, she took the second bottle of wine that had been opened and poured herself a hearty glass. Once Louisa was out of the room, she turned to look at Rex. "Cheers." She chugged half of it. "I should have left when you shut the cabin door on me."

"I would have still come." He joined her in more vino. "I needed to do this as much for me as for her."

"Okay, but we wouldn't have had sex last night, which opened up this crazy can of worms."

"My mother doesn't know we had sex. She's just—"

"I do now," Louisa said, pushing her IV pole through the dining room. "I forgot my cheaters. Can't see a damn thing without them."

Tilly dropped her head to the table and groaned. A wave of nausea flowed from her toes to her brain.

"You might as well share a room. I have no issue with that out of wed—"

"Louisa," Gerry said sternly. "Leave them alone."

"Good idea," Rex said. "I think we've all embarrassed Tilly enough for one night."

Tilly kept her head down, breathing deeply so she didn't hyperventilate. This was worse than getting caught with her hand in Rex's pants when they'd been in high school.

"Everyone's gone." Rex brushed her hair to the side, tracing his finger across her neck. "For the record, I thought you'd want to keep the tattoo to yourself, which is why I took your hair down. But you pushed my buttons, so I pushed back."

"They've all seen it. Made their comments. Trust me. I've been dealing with this longer than you have."

"So, I just made it all worse."

She bolted upright. "It wasn't just the letting my hair down thing, but you made a sexual innuendo—"

"I know. I'm sorry. It's just that it does really make my mother happy, and I've come to realize I've caused her so much pain. I'm trying to make it up to her."

"I'm glad. Really I am, and I'm willing to play along. Just we don't have to take it that far, much less announce what happened last night."

"That was a mistake," he said. "Come on. Let's take this outside and sit by the pool." He snagged the bottle of red. "We can discuss a plan that will satisfy my mother's need for us to be together, but with the boundaries you want."

"We're going to have to fake date until she dies, and this goes under the inappropriate category, but

I think you coming home might have extended her life indefinitely."

He laced his fingers through hers.

She told herself it was just practice. The only problem with that was how much she liked practicing.

"We only have to date when I'm home, and while I can take time off from the Aegis Network indefinitely, the fire station poses a different set of problems. I will have to change some shifts around, but we have one person out with injuries and others who are on vacation. I will have to go back and forth."

She glanced up at him. "You'd do that for your mother?"

"I was wrong to cut her out."

She plopped herself on a lounge chair, making sure her drink didn't spill, which was amazing considering how tipsy she was. Rex was turning out to be the same man she'd fallen in love with. Not the jerk that took off.

Go figure.

"Why, Rex Jordan, I think you might have grown up," she said.

"Don't tell anyone. I'd like to keep it a secret." He sat on the foot of the chair, swirling his glass.

"We're going to have to been seen in public, at the club. Are you ready for that?"

"I've already gotten two texts congratulating me on our recent reunion."

He shook his head. "I played golf with Eddy and his dad, both asking when the wedding will be."

"What have we gotten ourselves into?"

7

Rex spent the first night in his mother's house tossing and turning. Every time he got up to use the bathroom, he hoped he'd run into Tilly, but it never happened.

And he couldn't bring himself to sneak into her room. Things had gotten too weird. He needed to spend some time alone with her, without the premise of making his mother happy. So, with that in mind, he'd borrowed a buddy's sailboat, and he and Tilly would spend the day on the Chesapeake before being put on display at the club during an annual Tuesday evening couples' night, golf and all.

"You and boats," she said as he stepped on the twenty-foot day sailor. "You should have joined the Navy."

"Their firefighter program isn't as intense as the Air Force."

"Perhaps, but their white dress uniforms are smoking hot."

"You women love a man in uniform." He untied the boat after starting the single engine. It wasn't the windiest day, and he probably wouldn't even put the sail up. Hell, floating and drinking a few beers seemed more like a plan than anything else.

She'd removed her T-shirt, showing off a tiny bikini top. The sexy miniskirt made the outfit complete. Talk about smoking hot. She burned his lips every time he kissed her. She never understood how sexy she was, even now. She might carry herself with confidence, but that came because she knew she was smart. In the looks department, she always saw herself as just another pretty girl, nothing special.

She was special in every way.

"How was breakfast with your mother?" she asked, leaning back on the bench on the starboard side.

"She was disappointed you didn't join us."

"I went to yoga class, like I do every day I'm at her house." She covered her eyes with her hand, glancing in his direction. "Did she bring up the sleeping arrangements?"

"And then some." He shook his head. "My mom was always direct. Hell, she made me blush giving me the sex talk, trying to explain why I should listen to what a woman wanted and if that wasn't bad enough, she gave a few graphic details about how to please a woman. I wanted to crawl in a hole and die."

"Well, you must have listened to her at some point, because you always knew what I wanted and from the start, you knew what to do."

He laughed. "You never gave me a choice. Always so demanding in bed."

"I most certainly am not."

"Whatever you say." He steered the boat out into the Chesapeake, enjoying the hot summer sun beating down on his face. Not much different than being at home, except for Tilly, only he felt as if she belonged with him out on the boat.

That was a crazy thought.

He pulled the throttle back, slowing the boat into an alcove they used to hang out in back in the day. "Let's relax here." He shut the engine down and tossed over the anchor, securing the boat between a half dozen other boats enjoying the day.

"Wow, this brings back memories," she said as she smoothed out two towels. "We had a lot of fun here."

"We sure did." He sat down next to her and opened the cooler. "Look at all the kids in these boats."

"I know. We look like a couple of old farts."

"We are old farts." He twisted off the cap from a beer and handed it to her.

"Why'd you bring me here?"

"It seemed like a nice place to spend the day and talk without being scrutinized by everyone our parents know." He leaned back on his elbows.

"Speaking of parents, my mother texted, and she's bringing her new boyfriend to the club tonight."

"Great. She never liked me much." Before the affair, he'd gotten along with Mr. Bettencourt well enough, but Mrs. Bettencourt terrified him. She'd always give him this narrowed expression when he'd come pick up Tilly for a date.

Tilly sipped her beer, lifting her head toward the sun. "It wasn't you she didn't like. It was what she read in my diary that pissed her off."

"Good Lord." He shook his head. "Do I even want to know?"

"Let's just say that she read about our first time and was mortified."

"I never want to see your mother again," he muttered.

"She was impressed that you took care of all the precautions and called me the next morning to make sure I was okay. She did know you treated me well. And if it makes you feel any better, she doesn't like anyone whose penis I've touched."

He raised his longneck. "I don't want to hear about that. I don't like those pricks either."

She clanked her bottle with his. "I can't say I'm thrilled to know about all the skanky bitches you've had either."

The strange turn of events his life had taken over the last twenty-four hours felt more like the Twilight Zone than reality. "So, we're both jealous and miserable, relationship-wise, and yet we're more awkward with each other than that pimply teenaged boy over there trying to feel up the blonde who seems so into him, only he's too hormonal to know it."

"Oh my God. That's almost exactly what I said to you when I first kissed you."

"My mother always liked how aggressive you were, which still weirds me out."

Tilly tilted her head and peered over her sunglasses.

"Well, you were aggressive," he said.

"Only in response to you," she whispered, brushing her hair from her face. "I'm sorry about your mom. She's a good woman. I didn't make things easy on her and my dad when we first moved in. But she's been good to me and I wish things were different."

"So do I," he admitted. His mother's illness had been another reason that had kept him up the night before.

His mom had put on a brave front, but after talking with her doctor this morning, Rex had a much better idea of how sick she really was. She had days, or at best, a couple of weeks before her organs went into failure. The cancer had eaten up all of her insides, leaving her with nothing but sickness.

He'd called Arthur right after and begged him to find replacements for his shifts. Timothy at the Aegis Network had told him not to worry. No assignments would be sent his way until he was ready.

"What are you thinking about?"

"I've missed out on so much. My sister is still

mad as hell at me, but says she'll be coming over tomorrow night for dinner. My brother and his family are coming too, which will be nice."

"That will really make your mother happy. I'll make sure I have plans."

"Not a good idea. My mom wants you there. I actually think she believes we'll make the announcement of our engagement."

"That would give *my* mother a heart attack."

"Doesn't she know this is all fake dating? That we are just pretending for the sake of my mother?"

Tilly shook her head, biting down on her lower lip. Never a good sign.

"Wonderful. So, she thinks we're getting back together as well."

"I'd be lying if I didn't say she's hopeful. She thinks my dating record has gone downhill since you, which is funny, considering she used to tell me I could do better than you."

He winked. "Boyfriends don't come any better than me."

She cocked her head. "You're a conceited ass." She slapped his shoulder, letting her fingers linger over their shared tattoo.

"Oh, for fuck's sake. I can't take it anymore." He pointed to the kids on the boat next to them.

The young boy kept trying to get closer to the girl on the deck. "We need to give that boy a hand."

"How do you suppose we do that?"

Rex whistled. "Hey. Do either of you have a cell phone we can use? Ours are dead, and I need to let a buddy of ours know where we are."

Tilly leaned closer. "What are you doing?" she whispered.

"Helping a brother out."

"Sure," the boy yelled.

"This is going to be fun." Rex dove into the water, swimming toward the kid's boat. As a kid, boy, he had no game. If it wasn't for Tilly and her ability to sweep him off his feet, he would have never asked her out.

Now all he had to do was put some helpful notes about dating on the teenager's phone, get the kid's number, and shoot him some texts while he watched and hopefully the poor boy wouldn't crash and burn.

"I really appreciate this," Rex said as he pushed himself up, sitting on the stern swim platform, taking the phone the boy offered. "Your phone or hers?"

"Mine," the boy said, glancing over his shoulder.

The young girl lay on the bow with earbuds, her feet tapping away. First Rex punched in his number, sending himself a text, then he opened the notes tab on the phone.

You want help with making a move on the girl? Just watch and follow what I do.

He handed the phone back, with the notes facing the boy who squinted and gave Rex a funny look. He realized he must have really looked like a creeper, but hopefully the boy would take notice.

Rex dove back into the water. The cool feel of the ocean rolled over his skin. He eyed Tilly, who sat, hugging her knees, smiling.

God, what a fool he'd been for twelve fucking years.

"Seriously, what did you do?" Tilly asked, handing him a towel.

"I told him to follow exactly what I do, so whatever you do, don't hit me and when I lean in to kiss you, make it look good."

"I don't think I can do that. I mean, you're such a terrible kisser." She rolled her eyes.

He smiled, but what he really wanted to do was draw her in by her hips and plant a wet one on her right now, but he'd have to wait.

They sat on the bow, cross-legged, watching the

young couple, waiting for the right moment, which came when the girl sat up.

Rex noticed the kid glancing his way, so he raised a hand, brushing a piece of hair from Tilly's face, dropping his finger to her shoulder and gliding it across her skin.

"Wow, the boy's mimicking you."

"Good," he whispered, sliding his finger back up, doing a little circle on the top of her shoulder. "Too bad the kid can't hear what I'm about to whisper in your ear." He leaned in, feeling the warmth of her skin against his lips. "You're more beautiful than the sun's rays dancing over the water."

"Good line," she said.

He kissed her cheek. "You're making my heart melt."

"Oh, look, he just did what you did and… oh, wow, she's aggressive."

"What's she doing?"

"This." Tilly wrapped her arms around him, smacking her mouth against his while her tongue swirled around, making him dizzy with desire.

"My job here is done." He leaned back on his hands, stretching his legs. The young couple across from them continued to kiss for a little while longer, then giggled and laughed and kissed some more.

"I would have never thought to do that," she said.

"What? Kiss me?"

She tilted her head. "You know what I meant."

He nodded. "But you're thinking about kissing me now."

"That one beer must have gone straight to your head."

He lay on his back, staring up at her. "Maybe, but I'm hoping after our date tonight, I'll get to feel you up like I did the night of the end of the summer fireworks."

She slapped his arm. "You're impossible."

"I know." He closed his eyes, letting the rocking of the boat gently lull him. If this boat had a bed, he'd be leading her to the cuddy and using his best moves to get her to sleep with him again.

His heart wasn't melting anymore.

No. His heart burned with the need to be with her again.

To love her.

It was crazy. He didn't know if it was being back and the nostalgia of it all.

Or if it was real.

But he wanted to find out.

"You're a good man," she whispered.

He blinked open an eye as she spread out her blanket.

She lay on her stomach, propped up on her elbows, staring off into the bay. There were many days and nights he'd thought about her and what she might be doing. Or what it might be like to be with her again.

But they were fleeting thoughts. Memories of a time he couldn't allow himself to fully enjoy because he was too much of an asshole.

"If that were true, I would have come home a long time ago."

She brushed her warm lips over his shoulder. "Don't let guilt start filling up your heart. Let's get through this these next few weeks of making your mom happy and healing all these wounds. After that, we can all walk away knowing we did right by her and maybe we can be friends."

Friends.

He wasn't sure that was going to be enough.

8

Tilly's knee jumped wildly under the table. Not even Rex's steady hand could calm her nerves.

"That last putt of yours was amazing," James, her mother's new boyfriend, said.

"He was always quite the golfer," her mother said with a smile. For a woman who hadn't liked Rex that much, she certainly had a thing for him now. She'd being hanging on him like he was the best thing since sliced bread the entire round. It was almost disgusting to watch. "I'm so sad your father and his new bride couldn't join us."

Rex loosened the tie around his neck before taking another large sip of wine. He'd never been one to enjoy wearing what he called a noose. He hated the damn things. He didn't mind golf clothes, but suits made the man practically break out in hives. "My mother wasn't feeling too well, so they decided it was best to stay home."

"I'm so sorry," her mother said, shaking her head. "Your mother's a good woman and I wish this wasn't happening. She's been through so much. First her son not speaking to—"

"Mom," Tilly interrupted. "Can we please not go there. Rex is here now."

"Yes. He is, and that says something." Her mother let out a long breath. "So, tell me, Rex, what exactly are your intentions with my daughter?"

"Mom, really, I'm not twelve."

"It's all right. I suspect if I had a child, I'd be the same way." Rex set his glass down. "It's been a long time and a lot of feelings have been hurt. Right now, it's all about reconnecting. I never stopped caring for your daughter and my mother's illness has reminded me how short life is."

Tilly coughed. The man could act. It was an Oscar worthy performance. She wished she had the ability to do it as well as he did. But her emotions were raw. They swirled around in her gut, smacking her heart, reminding her that when all this was over, Rex would be gone.

Sure, he wouldn't be out of their lives. Not this time. He'd be coming around to see his father. His brother and his family. His sister.

But outside of that, the pretending would end and she would go back to her life without him being a staple in it.

"That's all well and good, but you made my little girl cry and I'd hate to go through that again."

"Oh my God, Mother. This has to stop. Can we just have a nice dinner and not rehash the past?"

"But if you two are getting back together—"

"Mrs. Bettencourt." Rex put his hand over her mother's. "I have no intention of making Tilly cry. That's the last thing I want. Right now, we're simply dating, getting to know one another again. I don't know where it will lead. I just know I want the opportunity to explore the possibilities and Tilly seems to want the same thing." He turned and caught her gaze. "Right? That is what you want."

Nothing like putting her on the spot with a big old hot truth, but told in the form of a lie, because Rex was just putting on a good show.

"Yes. That's what I want." She did her best to

smile, but she wondered if her face contorted like she'd just ate a lemon.

"Here comes the waiter with our appetizers," James said, resting his arm around the back of her mother's chair. "Sweetheart, I think you've put enough pressure on these kids. You heard them, now it's time to leave them alone and let them figure things out."

Her mother pursed her lips. "I only want to see my little girl happy again and all she's done for the last twelve years—"

"Darling, not the time or place," James said.

Thank God for James.

Her mother jerked her head. "Why not? I know I promised I'd be on my best behavior and I have been. I've bit my tongue and only glossed over the past." She turned her gaze toward Rex. "I'm not sure you understand the mess you left behind."

"That's enough, Mother," Tilly said under her breath.

"It's okay, Tilly." Rex took her hand. "I'm well aware of what I did. To my family and to Tilly and I'm sorry. I know those are only words. It's my actions that need to speak."

Her mother nodded. "I don't mean to be so hard

on you. But I know your mother. Pretty well. We've been through being friends. Being mortal enemies." Her mother lowered her chin. "To coming together again, creating peace for the sake of all our children. That included you. So, excuse me for trying to poke holes in this newfound relationship."

"What are you implying, Mother?" Tilly should have known. Her mother sometimes could be the most untrusting human being on the planet. Life had given her some hard knocks and for a few years after the divorce, she didn't trust a single soul. Not even her own kids. When Tilly moved in with her dad and Louisa, her mom accused her of being a rat leaving a sinking ship.

That wasn't the case. But she understood why her mom would feel that way.

"I know you still care about Rex. I get that. I want to know that he's not playing some silly game to make his mother happy. There. I said it. Sorry. But Louisa has always wanted the two of you back together." Her mother lifted her wineglass and took a long sip.

"So have you," James said. "And don't you dare go lying about it, because I'll call you on it." He arched a brow.

"We're not talking about me right now, are we?" She took another gulp.

Rex squeezed Tilly's hand. "I can assure you this isn't a game and I'm not playing at anything. I love my mother and I'd do almost anything for her, but I care about Tilly. That's a fact. I honestly want to get to know her again and am grateful she's giving me the chance." He reached across the table and filled his plate with a couple of shrimp.

This was such a bad idea. Everyone was going to get hurt in the end.

Especially her.

———

Tilly tossed her purse on the dresser, then fell backward onto the soft, plush bed, exhausted after the evening with her wacko mother.

The second they'd walked in the door, Rex had been called to see his mother. She'd had a rough day, pain-wise, but also, the day nurse said Louisa had taken a turn for the worse. Tilly feared the end was sooner than everyone thought.

Louisa put on a brave face every day and was a true fighter. One of the strongest women Tilly had ever known.

A couple of light knocks came from the bathroom. She rolled her head and there stood Rex in the same light-blue button-down shirt and pair of dark slacks. The only thing missing was his tie.

"Is your mom okay?"

"She's resting a little more comfortably right now. The doctor will be over in the morning, but he thinks we should take her to the hospital. He doesn't believe she has much time left. Days maybe."

"She wants to stay home and die here."

"I know. I told her I wouldn't make her go." He leaned against the doorjamb. "Is that the right decision?"

"I think so." Tilly scooted up to the head of the bed. "All they will do in the hospital is manage her pain, which we are doing here, but she won't have the comforts of home."

He shoved his hands in his pockets, staring at her intently.

"Something wrong?"

He sauntered across the room, kicked off his shoes, and stood at the end of the bed. Curling his fingers around her ankles, he yanked her toward him. Her dress slid up her thighs and over her butt, exposing her tiny thong. Her breathing became erratic as her chest heaved. She opened her mouth, but no words came out, only a lust-filled groan.

He dropped to his knees, leaned forward, and kissed her passionately through her cotton panties. There was no foreplay. No teasing. He went right for the prize.

She should stop him. He didn't want her; he wanted to bury his pain inside someone. Anyone would probably do. She understood the pain of losing a parent. When her father died, all she wanted was for someone to hold her. Love her.

She'd wanted Rex and wished he'd come for her.

But he didn't.

Not even when she wrote him and begged.

He pushed the fabric to the side and slipped in two fingers. Her body was already wet with antici-pation. She clung to the bedsheets, digging her heels into the mattress. Whatever he needed, she'd give it to him if it eased a tiny bit of his suffering.

As he pulled her panties off, a ripple of heartache washed over her. She'd let him take her because she was selfish. She wanted to have him as many times as she could, no matter the cost to her heart. She tried to tell herself she was doing this for him. Helping him ease his grief of reconnecting with his mother, only to lose her in death days later.

She understood guilt and grief and the turmoil that it could create in a person's soul.

He nestled himself between her legs, kissing and sucking. Her hips rolled involuntarily with the gentle gliding of his fingers. He kissed her passionately as if he were kissing her mouth. His hands massaged her thighs. His normal earnestness was replaced with tenderness. There was no desperation in his touch. No raw animal desire.

Just sweet love.

She gasped, resisting the urge to clutch his head and grind herself against him.

His tongue floated across her like a feather drifting in the air. The room spun as an orgasm erupted inside her like a volcano. Her body trembled, and she struggled to catch her breath. He kissed her stomach, pushing himself off the bed.

She watched him undress in silence as she removed her dress, tossing it haphazardly to the floor, their normal banter replaced with unspoken words. His gaze roamed her body like a knife gliding through a decadent piece of chocolate cake.

For the first time with him, she had no idea

what to do, so she lay there, waiting, letting him take his fill of her body.

Her pulse beat out of control, and she began to wonder if he was even going to climb back on the bed and make love to her.

Make love.

The concept tore through her mind. Their sex had always been playful. It wasn't that they hadn't once loved each other, but sex wasn't necessarily how they conveyed the strong emotion with one another. It was an act of pleasure.

He finally made his way back to the bed, climbing between her legs, the length of him throbbing against her thighs. He planted his elbows next to her ears, his hands cupping her face as he stared into her eyes. Saying nothing, he slowly shifted, sinking himself into her.

She dug her fingers into his shoulders, holding on for dear life. Blinking, she managed to keep the tears stinging her eyes from breaking free.

She loved him.

Never stopped.

Never would.

But she'd never have him. Once his mother passed, he'd go back to Florida. He wouldn't ask her to go with him. She knew that for a fact. And she couldn't beg him to stay.

They were right back where they had left off twelve years ago, and there would be no happy ending.

His lips brushed gently over hers as his hips rose up and down in a soft rolling motion like waves crashing at the shoreline.

Her back involuntarily arched into him, her soft moans gaining in strength. She felt every inch of him swell deep inside. Her eyes remained locked with his mesmerizing stare. Biting down on her lip, a second climax shook her and with it he tenderly kissed her lips. His breath labored as his movements increased in both speed and intensity. His eyes widened as a deep guttural groan vibrated from his chest.

His body tightened as he thrust once, his release spilling out inside her.

No condom.

What a horrible thought to have right at this moment. She quickly pushed it aside, rubbing her hands up and down his back, rocking her hips slightly, enjoying the way his pupils dilated, then contracted as he orgasmed.

He kissed her nose and then collapsed on top of

her. She gladly accepted his weight, gently stroking his shoulders.

She held him like that for another ten minutes before he rolled to his side, tucking himself up behind her, holding her in his arms. In minutes, he was fast asleep.

Closing her eyes, she let out a long breath.

"I love you," she whispered so quietly that she barely heard the words herself.

He certainly hadn't, because if he had, he would have leaped from the bed and run for cover.

9

Tilly peeked open her eyes, the morning sunlight shining through the window. She blinked a few times, gaining focus.

"What time is it?" she asked.

No response.

She'd never been one to sleep in, and she hadn't known Rex to either.

Stretching, she rolled over, reaching out for him and got nothing but an empty bed.

She bolted upright, clutching the covers over her bare chest.

"Rex?" she called.

Looking around the room, she noticed his clothes had been picked up.

Her heart sank. He'd snuck out.

She'd woken up alone.

Again.

That shouldn't be an issue. He must have gotten up and decided to let her sleep. That would be the normal thing to do, not to think he'd taken off in the middle of the night.

Quickly, she got dressed in a pair of cotton shorts and a tank top. Deciding to check to see if he was in his room, she knocked on the door from inside the bathroom.

Silence.

She pushed open the door with a shaky hand and a pounding heart.

The bed was perfectly made, which she expected since he'd slept with her last night. She walked around the room and realized his suitcase was gone.

She sucked in her lower lip. A combination of rage and sorrow flowed through her body.

How could he just up and leave not just her, but his mother?

She raced through the house, making her way downstairs and into the kitchen where Gerry and Judy sat at the table, hovering over a couple mugs of coffee.

"Where's Rex?"

"He left a note saying he had to go to Florida to take care of something," Gerry said, glancing over his shoulder.

"When is he coming back?"

"The note said he'd be in touch," Judy said as she stood. "Can I make you some breakfast?"

She shook her head. "Be in touch? What does that mean? Does Louisa know?"

"Yes. He visited with her briefly this morning." Judy laced her fingers over Tilly's biceps. "She's not doing well. The doctor just left, and he said her kidneys aren't functioning. He believes she'll slip into a coma soon."

"And Rex left after hearing that? Unbelievable. What an asshole."

Judy jerked her hand back. "He's coming back."

"Right," Tilly said in a huff. He'd left once before without every looking back. He could easily do it again. "Where is the note?"

"I tossed it," Gerry said with a questioning tone. "Honey, what's going on?"

"Nothing."

Only everything.

A tear rolled down her cheek.

"Something has your feathers in a tailspin."

Gerry pulled out a chair. "Sit down and tell us what happened."

She sucked in a deep breath and leaned against the counter, wiping her face. This was not something she could do sitting down.

"I don't think I should be here when he comes back."

"Why do you say that?" Gerry asked. "Did you get into a fight?"

No. We made love. I told him I loved him, but he doesn't love me, so he bolted.

"Not a fight so much, but I don't belong here with him right now. I'm sure he sent me a text message or something asking me to leave before he gets back."

"I don't think my son would do that," Gerry said defensively.

She wanted to lay into him about how no one knew Rex anymore and remind him of the pain Rex had left in his wake twelve years ago. "He needs time to be with you and his mom. He doesn't need me."

"What about Louisa?" Judy asked with a furrowed brow. "She would be so sad if you left."

"I'll be back to visit, but I'm going to move back into my apartment."

The room filled with a deafening silence. When Rex had left the last time, he'd given her an ultimatum. He told her if she didn't go with him, he would never return for her, ever.

He left the next day.

Maybe he'd be back for his mom, but if he wanted her here, he would have woken her up and told her, left a note, or at worst, sent her a text.

"I'm going to go visit with Louisa, and then I'm going to pack my things." She straightened her spine and sucked in her pride.

Maybe getting over him would be easier the second time.

———

Rex tossed his suitcase in the back of Arthur's Jeep. "Thanks for picking me up."

"No problem. Nice jet."

"I prefer flying coach."

"I doubt that." Arthur pulled out of the airport, heading toward the marina. "How's your mom?"

"Not well at all."

"So, why are you here instead of being with her?"

"I need to get the ring," he said, tripping on the

last word. He'd woken up around three in the morning with Tilly in his arms, her hair pooled over his chest, the golden locks glistening in the moonlight. His heart had been beating out of control, and all he could think about was spending the rest of his life trying to make up for the past and giving her everything she wanted and needed.

"What ring?"

"My mother's ring." Rex rubbed his shaky hand over his thigh.

"I'm sorry, I don't follow."

Rex stared out the window at the Intracoastal Waterway. He'd give up his boat and the Aegis Network be with Tilly. He could be a firefighter anywhere, and he wanted to be where she was. "My mother, in an attempt to get me to come home years ago, sent me her engagement ring and told me how crushed Tilly had been when I left."

"So, your mom wants the ring?"

"No. It's not for my mom. It's for Tilly." The bubble of fear he'd been feeling blossomed into a blooming flower.

"Why? Does your mom want her to have it?"

"For a married man, you're really fucking clueless."

Arthur turned into the marina parking lot, glancing in his direction.

He smiled. "I'm going to ask Tilly to marry me."

Arthur let up on the clutch while still in gear, lurching the car forward. "Well, why are you sitting here? Get your ass in gear, and I'll drive you back to the airport."

Rex didn't waste any time, snagging his suitcase and racing down the dock like a lunatic. He didn't know when he'd come back, so he needed to pack more clothes. He'd been given time off for as long as he needed. Tears welled in his eyes. His mother wouldn't last long. Maybe a week, but hopefully she'd get to see her ring on Tilly's finger.

Once on the boat, he went straight to the safe. The hole in his heart slowly mended, but a prickle of fear that she'd say no troubled him deeply. He also had to make it clear that this wasn't for his mother, and even though he was rushing it, he knew without a doubt that he loved Tilly and wanted to spend the rest of his life with her.

There was no other woman for him. He'd tried relationships in the past, but they weren't Tilly.

He pulled out the pouch. He didn't even want to

look at it until he could ask Tilly. He stuffed it in his front pocket. As quickly as he could, he packed his larger suitcase and made a beeline to Arthur's car.

The entire ride to the airport, and subsequent flight, his heart fluttered, and his palms grew sweaty. His mind fast-forwarded to what he thought a life with her would be like.

When the limo pulled into the driveway of his mother's house, the gravity of what he was about to do sucker punched his ability to move. He sat in the back of the car feeling slightly nauseous, and a crushing pain slammed into his chest. For the last ten hours, he'd focused on the future and hadn't given a single thought as to how he would propose.

"I need to go to a florist right away," he told the driver.

10

Tilly stepped from the front door just as the limo pulled in. Gerry had told her that Rex was on his way back, and she just wanted to set the record straight. That she was okay and that when enough time had passed, they could close the book in their fake reunion. But she wasn't going to get the chance because the limo backed up and drove away.

Hurt quickly turned to anger.

She stood outside, trying to control her raging pulse, but no amount of deep breathing would help, so she tried pacing in the front yard.

That only made it worse.

Fifteen minutes after the limo left, she stormed

back into the house and slammed the door, rattling the painting on the wall.

"Tilly," Judy said from the sitting room, tipping her head and glaring at her over her cheaters as she continued her knitting. "That was totally uncalled for."

Tilly no longer cared what his family thought. "Rex took one look at me and turned around and left." She pulled her phone from her back pocket and pulled up his contact information.

"I doubt that, dear," Judy said.

"Well, that's what he did." She started to send a nasty text but then decided he wasn't worth it if he couldn't even get out of the car and face her.

"What happened between the two of you?" Judy set her yarn on her lap.

"We found out the hard way that we aren't a good fit."

"Oh," Judy said, setting her glasses down. "I see."

"It doesn't matter and honestly, I think this actually gives us closure." She rubbed the back of her neck. "I'm going to get my things and head to my apartment."

"Wait until after dinner. Rex's sister and brother will be here. I'm sure they will want to see you."

Both Emily and Miles had been supportive of Tilly over the years, but she didn't need to be around them tonight. "It's really best if I go. It should just be immediate family right now."

"You're immediate family," Gerry said as he waltzed into the room.

"No. I'm not."

He rested his hand on her shoulder. "I really don't know happened, but I just got off the phone with Rex. I told him you thought he left because of you and—"

"Gerry, why would you say that?" she screeched.

"Because I don't understand why you're so upset." He arched a brow. "He said he's sending the car back for you shortly."

"Why?" She looked at her phone and saw that Rex had texted her twice and called three times. She pulled up the messages.

Rex: *We need to talk. Sending car back for you.*

Rex: *Are you there? I've called and called. This is important. Please. Answer me.*

The honking of a horn startled her.

"The car is here," Gerry said.

She swallowed, looking out the window at the

stretch limo. The driver stood outside, his hand on the rear passenger door.

"Go," Judy said, waving her hand. "Whatever it is, don't you think you owe it to yourself to find out?"

"No," she said.

Gerry took her by the forearms. "You and Rex are so stubborn. And sometimes so much so you can't see straight. Just do it. See what he has to say and you can say your piece as well."

She sucked in a deep breath. "Fine." She took slow tentative steps toward the vehicle. The driver opened the door, and she slipped inside, half wishing Rex was inside so she could just get this over with and leave. "Where are we going?"

"I've been asked to take you to the club."

"The club? Why?"

"That's just what I was told."

She leaned back, folding her arms over her chest. Nothing made sense anymore. She wanted to go back to when she'd been given the choice to leave him on his boat. He said he would have come anyway, so that first night wouldn't have happened, and neither would last night have.

The ride to the club took all of ten minutes. She was greeted by a young bag boy in a golf cart.

"Mr. Jordan is waiting on the ninth green."

"Why?" She stared at the young boy who had the stupidest grin plastered on his face.

"I'm not at liberty to say."

As they rode across the golf course, the golfers stepped to the side, pointing and waving. They rolled down the eighth fairway and all she could think about was their first kiss, right there on the ninth green.

What the hell was he up to?

Her heart hammered against her chest. Through the trees, she saw Rex standing at that very spot, roses in hand.

"Turn this sucker around," she whispered. The last time Rex had given her roses was the first night they'd slept together. He hadn't done it since, saying that roses were only for the most special of occasions and then teased her that she wouldn't be getting them from him again unless he were to propose.

"Are you serious?" the bag boy asked with a high-pitched squeak.

"Yes. No. I don't know," she muttered. No way could he be asking her that. Maybe he was just going to apologize for being an asshole. She could deal with that.

The kid pulled the cart up next to Rex. The flowers in his hands shook.

"You made it," he said, holding out his hand.

She didn't take it. "What do you want, Rex?" Mentally, she beat the crap out of herself. Being a bitch wasn't going to help the situation.

"Do you remember what happened here?" he asked. His voice had a funny tone to it.

"Our first kiss," she mumbled.

"That was mind-blowing."

"I suppose," she said, pinching herself, trying to change her attitude. He was making an effort. The least she could do was meet him halfway.

"Are you mad at me?" he asked.

"Ya think?"

He scowled. "Whatever I did to upset you, I'm very sorry."

"You left without saying goodbye and went back to Florida."

"I was there for an hour to get some—"

She held up her hand, painfully aware that a crowd of golfers had gathered in the distance. "You didn't wake me to tell me or leave me a note or even bother to text me. Considering our past history, what was I to think?"

"I left a note." He pinched his nose. "I said I'd be back."

"It felt like you snuck out. I don't mind being used, considering everything you're going through. I mean, I offered myself up to you, but you could have done the decent thing and—"

He cupped her mouth.

She batted it away. "Don't hush me." She wasn't about to be quiet now. He hadn't really apologized for anything and didn't even understand why she was upset, and she was going to tell him exactly what was on her mind.

"You're yelling on a golf course, and people are starting to stare."

"You brought me here." She planted her hands on her hips. "And I have a few things I want to say to you."

"This isn't going as I planned." He scratched the side of his face. "Here. These are for you." He held out the roses, which trembled in his hands. "I also have something I want to say."

"Why are we here?" She took the roses, lifting them to her nose and inhaling the fresh scent.

"I had this whole thing planned to ask if you remembered our first kiss and the first time we…" He glanced around, and his cheeks flushed red.

She'd never seen him blush before. Ever.

"I remember the first time vividly," she whispered. Her throat dried up, and she could barely swallow. "I appreciate the gesture, but I'm tired of the—"

"I gave you roses."

She nodded.

"Do you remember what I said about roses?"

"Oh my God. You can't be serious?" She reached out and clutched the nearest tree. "This is all just for show, right? For your mom, right? Give a dying woman her wish? Jesus, Rex. I can't do this."

"Tilly, I'm sorry that me leaving last night upset you. Or that you didn't see my note and that this isn't going the way I envisioned, but this isn't for show. If it was, I would have done it in front of my mother." He lifted her chin with his thumb. "I'm not a flowers kind of guy. I'm certainly not a romantic."

"No, you most certainly are not. And you have a weird sense of humor."

"I'm not laughing," he said. "I love you, Tilly. I always have. I'm sorry that me racing off to get my mother's ring hurt you—"

"Ring?" She dropped the flowers. Her muscles felt like jelly. "What ring?"

"My mother's ring," he said.

"What do you mean? What ring?"

"Her engagement ring, and she sent it to me years ago. I don't know why I kept it. I thought about sending it back to her, but never did," he said. "It was on my boat in Florida and I couldn't propose without it. That's why I went back. I had to get it."

"This isn't happening," she whispered, staring into his smoldering eyes.

"Do you love me, Tilly?"

She blew out a puff of air. "I never stopped."

He lowered himself to one knee.

She clutched her necklace, staring down at him holding out a diamond—a huge diamond ring.

"The second you stepped onto my boat, I couldn't deny any more how much I missed you. I'm not going to give you any kind of ultimatum. I can be a firefighter anywhere. It doesn't have to be in Jacksonville and the Aegis Network is constantly expanding. Maybe they would let me—"

"I can't let you give up your life's work for me."

"I can and I will. But know if you shoot me down today." He took her hand and dropped his forehead to it. "Which I hope you don't, I will stick it out and fight for us this time."

"You're really asking me to marry you?" A wide smile tugged at the corners of her mouth. Her heart fluttered, and she felt like she was floating on air.

"Yes."

"That's my line," she said.

He slipped the ring on her finger and kissed her hand. "Is that a yes?"

"Can I think about it?"

He stood, taking her into his strong, protective arms. "You're killing me here."

"I love you, Rex Jordan, and I'm never going to let you go. Not now. Not ever. You're stuck with me now." She pressed her lips against his, listening to the cheers in the background.

"I love you," he whispered in ear. "I have one more thing to ask you."

"What's that?"

"Can we get married right away? I know you probably want the white dress, big wedding—"

"We can get a marriage license tomorrow and since this is because you want your mother there, I'm sure she'd let us have a small ceremony at the house."

A golfer in the distance yelled, "Fore!"

They climbed up on the back of the golf cart.

"I'm not letting you leave the life you carved out with your buddies in Florida."

"We can figure all that out later," he said. "But there is something else I'd like to ask you."

"Yeah, what's that?"

"How do you feel about having a family of our own?"

She bit down on her lower lip. "We were careless last night."

He shrugged. "We're not getting any younger."

11

R ex stood at his mother's grave. Tears poured out his eyes like a waterfall. He fiddled with his wedding ring, grateful his mom had lasted long enough to see him marry the love of his life.

Tilly leaned against his arm, resting her head on his shoulder. "She died knowing she brought love and peace. That's all she wanted."

He swiped at his cheeks. "I wish I could have given her more."

"Don't go to that place," Tilly whispered. "All wrongs have been righted."

"I know, babe." He kissed her temple. "Are you sure moving to Jacksonville is what you want?"

"We can come home and visit family anytime

we want." She smiled. "It's time for me to shift gears. Starting my own foundation is something I've always wanted to do. It's easier for me to pack up my life. But you can't pack up your buddies." She pointed to his team who had all made the trip to his mother's funeral. "I'm not going to ask you to turn your back on them, and before you start in on me about the idea I might be giving up something, I'm not. Neither of us is giving the other an ultimatum this time. We're doing what's best for us. For our family." She turned, taking his hand and placing it on her belly. "My only regret is that I didn't have the chance to tell your mother that her little boy's going to be a daddy."

"I'm going to be a what?" He jerked his head back.

Tilly smiled, pressing his hand harder against his middle. "That's right, big fella. Me throwing up and feeling sick all the time hasn't been from the stress of everything that's been going on. It's because I'm pregnant."

"Well, I'll be damned. Wait until the guys hear about this." He puffed out his chest. "My dad and Judy are going to go nuts and spoil this kid rotten."

"So are you."

"Did you hear that, Ma? Your baby boy's gonna

have a little one of his own." He looped his arm around her waist. "I hope it's a boy. That way I only have one penis to worry about."

Tilly laughed. "What are you going to do if it's a girl."

"Lock her up and throw away the key." He nudged Tilly toward the direction of the rest of his family and his friends. He never thought he'd see this day, but now that it was here, he knew this was exactly how his life was supposed to turn out. He reached inside his sport coat. "I have a surprise for you." He handed her an envelope.

"What's this?"

"Open it," he said.

She tore open the edges and glanced at the tickets inside. "Oh my," she whispered. "You're taking me to Greece?"

"On a proper honeymoon, since we didn't get to do that right after we got married." His mom had hung on for a week and a half after he and Tilly had tied the knot. He'd refused to leave her beside and Tilly hadn't once asked him to. He loved her even more for that.

"Good thing you like morning sex, because I feel like shit by four in the evening and thus far, chicken and coffee and make me want to stick my head in the sand."

"We can cancel if you want."

"Bite your tongue, husband." She hip checked him. "You'll just have to adjust your thinking and take me on romantic breakfasts instead of dinners."

"That can be arranged."

"Because you understand the word romantic." She laughed.

"I'm learning." He pulled her tighter. "Thank you for being you and waiting for me to get my shit together."

"I could say the same thing right back to you."

"I love you, Tilly, and I can't wait to see what gorgeous babies we make."

EPILOGUE

TWO YEARS LATER...

R ex pushed back the garage door to the home he and Tilly had bought not far from the marina. He'd made the decision to stay with the Aegis Network, and he fulfilled his dream to be an arson investigator with the local fire department. His assignments with the Aegis Network kept him closer to home, especially now that they had little Annabelle Louisa. His heart physically hurt just thinking about leaving her for any length of time.

Being at work during the day was hard enough.

"I hear Daddy," Tilly cooed.

"Da Da," Annabelle screamed as she wobbled down the hallway, her hands flapping in the air. At fifteen months, she was an inquisitive ball of energy. Just like her mother.

Being the father of a daughter was going to be the death of him, especially since she already showed signs of being *boy* crazy. All she talked about was little Tommy who lived next door.

"How's my baby girl?" He bent over and scooped her into his arms, brushing away her long blond locks, just like her mother.

"Good." She cupped his face with her pudgy little hands and pursed her lips. "Mommy had bad day."

"Oh no, what's happened?" Tilly had made the decision to create her own foundation to help create safe environments for women and children who suffered abuse. This had been a huge undertaking, but the millions of dollars they had between both families wasn't doing anyone any good sitting in some stock or bond.

"Mommy sick! She been on sofa and can't play with me."

"Then we best get inside and help her out tonight." He set Annabelle down, who went running off into the family room, bouncing twice off the walls, giggling all the way. She jumped on the couch where Tilly had stretched out her legs.

"Hey, babe, what's going on?"

"Not dinner," she said with a weak smile. "I feel like death."

"I think I can handle cooking tonight. Did you have something in mind?"

"I took out chicken, but when I was preparing it, I barfed." She cocked a brow.

"Stay away from me, then. Last thing I need is the stomach bug."

"You can't get this kind of ailment," she said, shifting to a sitting position. "Annabelle, will you go get Mommy the crackers?"

"All sicknesses are contagious." He sat down next to the woman who would forever rock his world, pressing the back of his hand on her cheek, but she didn't feel warm. "A few people have been out sick at the station. Something is going around."

"Morning sickness is not contagious."

"Ha ha. It's evening and… no." He dropped his hand to his thigh. "Seriously. We weren't even trying and you're pregnant?"

She nodded. "I took the test this morning when the smell of coffee made me want to puke my guts out. What is it with you? We go without birth control once or twice and I'm knocked up."

"We're going to have another kid?" He pointed

to Annabelle, who handed Tilly a sleeve of saltines. "Two of those little things bouncing around like basketballs?"

Annabelle jumped up on his lap. "What little things, Da Da? I'm not a ball. I'm a girl!"

"Mommy's going to have a baby." Tears stung the corners of his eyes. "What do you think about that, Annabelle?"

"Yay!" She kissed his lips before jumping down and running off toward her toys in the middle of the room. The kid couldn't sit still for a second.

He looped his arm around Tilly, pulling her close. "I'm sorry our babies make you sick."

"It's only for a few months," she said, smiling. "I'm more concerned about how you're going to be when she starts dating."

"I'll be fine, because she won't be allowed to date. Ever. No boy is going to try to kiss my little girl."

"Because she's going to take after her mother and kiss them first."

"That's what I'm afraid of," he muttered. "This one better be a boy so he can help me scare the crap out of her suitors, starting with little Tommy next door."

"Speaking of which, they have a playdate

tomorrow afternoon. Since you're off work and I'll be sick, you get to play chaperone." Tilly poked his arm. "And they're babies, so don't start with talk about how he can't date your daughter. It freaks people out."

"Yeah, well, they were playing doctor the other day. *That* freaked me out." He eased back onto the sofa, resting Tilly's head in his lap, stroking her long blond hair, while he watched his precious daughter play with her new favorite dolly. "They were running around in their diapers with—"

"That's normal, Rex. And someday she's going to grow up, fall in love with some amazing fellow like you—"

"Who broke her mother's heart like an asshole." He leaned over and kissed Tilly's forehead.

"Anyone ever tell you that you say the dumbest things sometimes?"

"Yeah, my wife. Every day."

Tilly laughed. "Are you ready to do this all over again?"

"About as ready as I'll ever be."

"Da Da!" Annabelle came rushing over. "Wanna play wedding? We can get married."

"Absolutely." Gently, he slipped from the sofa and scooped up his baby girl, twirling her around.

"Remember, someday when you're much older and some guy tries to take you away, I loved you first."

Thank you for taking the time to read REX'S HONOR. Please feel free to leave an honest review. Next up in the series is KENT'S HONOR.

Grab a glass of vino, kick back, relax, and let the romance roll in…

Sign up for my Newsletter (https://dl.bookfunnel.com/82gm8b9k4y) where I often give away free books before publication.

Join my private Facebook group (https://www.facebook.com/groups/191706547909047/) where I post exclusive excerpts and discuss all things murder and love!

ABOUT THE AUTHOR

Jen Talty is the *USA Today* Bestselling Author of Contemporary Romance, Romantic Suspense, and Paranormal Romance. In the fall of 2020, her short story was selected and featured in a 1001 Dark Nights Anthology.

Regardless of the genre, her goal is to take you on a ride that will leave you floating under the sun with warmth in your heart. She writes stories about broken heroes and heroines who aren't necessarily looking for romance, but in the end, they find the kind of love books are written about :).

She first started writing while carting her kids to one hockey rink after the other, averaging 170 games per year between 3 kids in 2 countries and 5 states. Her first book, IN TWO WEEKS was originally published in 2007. In 2010 she helped form a publishing company (Cool Gus Publishing) with *NY*

Times Bestselling Author Bob Mayer where she ran the technical side of the business through 2016.

Jen is currently enjoying the next phase of her life…the empty nester! She and her husband reside in Jupiter, Florida.

Grab a glass of vino, kick back, relax, and let the romance roll in…

Sign up for my Newsletter (https://dl.bookfunnel.com/ 82gm8b9k4y) where I often give away free books before publication.

Join my private Facebook group (https://www.facebook. com/groups/191706547909047/) where I post exclusive excerpts and discuss all things murder and love!

Never miss a new release. Follow me on Amazon:amazon.com/author/jentalty

And on Bookbub: bookbub.com/authors/jentalty

ALSO BY JEN TALTY

Brand new series: SAFE HARBOR!

Mine To Keep

Mine To Save

Mine To Protect

Mine to Hold

Mine to Love

Check out LOVE IN THE ADIRONDACKS!

Shattered Dreams

An Inconvenient Flame

The Wedding Driver

Clear Blue Sky

Blue Moon

Before the Storm

NY STATE TROOPER SERIES (also set in the Adirondacks!)

In Two Weeks

Dark Water

Deadly Secrets

Murder in Paradise Bay

To Protect His own

Deadly Seduction

When A Stranger Calls

His Deadly Past

The Corkscrew Killer

First Responders: A spin-off from the NY State Troopers series

Playing With Fire

Private Conversation

The Right Groom

After The Fire

Caught In The Flames

Chasing The Fire

Legacy Series

Dark Legacy

Legacy of Lies

Secret Legacy

Emerald City

Investigate Away

Sail Away

Georgia Moon

Jack Daniels

Jim Beam

Whiskey Sour

Whiskey Cobbler

Whiskey Smash

Irish Whiskey

The Monroes

Color Me Yours

Color Me Smart

Color Me Free

Color Me Lucky

Color Me Ice

Color Me Home

Search and Rescue

Protecting Ainsley

Protecting Clover

Protecting Olympia

Protecting Freedom

Protecting Princess

Protecting Marlowe

The Last Flight

The Return Home

The Matriarch

Aegis Network: Jacksonville Division

A SEAL's Honor

Talon's Honor

Arthur's Honor

Rex's Honor

Kent's Honor

Aegis Network Short Stories

Max & Milian

A Christmas Miracle

Spinning Wheels

Holiday's Vacation

The Brotherhood Protectors

Out of the Wild

Rough Justice

Rough Around The Edges

Rough Ride

Rough Edge

Rough Beauty